THE GLOVE

By David Farrell

For Tess

Here's to the future.

Time goes by in a haze of baby sized purchases and parenting classes. I read the books and we watch the YouTube videos. Sometimes we prepare together and sometimes apart. I do all the stuff they say you're meant to do before a baby invades your life. On paper we couldn't be more prepared but knowing we are about to become parents makes me uneasy. Most of my anxiety comes from the way life has changed since we found out. We haven't been the same. We're falling out of love with each other and neither of us cares enough to correct our course.

Sam and I are never affectionate anymore. We've stopped saying goodbye in the mornings. We've stopped kissing each other goodnight. She faces away from me as she sleeps and I can't tell how she feels anymore. I used to *know*. I didn't need to wonder. Maybe she would be better off without me. In all honesty I've considered leaving her during some of our colder nights. I imagine a life without her in it and that scares me. Imagining co-parenting a child scares me too.

I shouldn't have proposed. Now I'm worried that after this kid arrives we'll break up. I'm fairly sure we will, in fact. There doesn't seem to be another outcome. Why can't we just talk about our feelings? I'm not ready. I'm worried I'll never see this child again and effectively ruin its life with my absence. I never wanted children anyway. Why should I care now? The unspoken truth that stops me from running out the door is that deep down I want my kid to have a better life than I did. I'm sure that's what most parents want, right? Step one in making that happen is to actually stick around. Unless staying is going to do *more* damage in some unknowable way.

Following the wedding we stayed at the beach for two more nights. We said goodbye to Doug and Jessica, who drove off blissfully into the sunset to begin their marriage together. Doug hugged me tightly that morning and I felt pretty good about us being friends again. We haven't really spoken since that hug but I feel confident that we will see each other soon. I was happy to know I had my best friend back after all those silent years. Doug knew me in a way that Sam didn't. There was a comfort in our friendship that didn't exist in my relationship with Sam.

I'd been considering telling her all about my deviant past. I wanted to trust Sam and let her know everything. If she could know the worst things about me and still love me then maybe our future would be okay. Maybe I would have a renewed faith in what we were. But then everything changed. Sam dropped the pregnancy bombshell and I felt the foundation we'd built shatter under its weight. Now I just want to shut her out again.

Sam wanted to keep the baby, so an abortion was never an option. It was made clear to me that I didn't have any say. She couldn't tell that I was already starting to mentally pull away. The baby was going to be the only proof that anything ever existed between Sam and I. This was the first time Sam had ever been pregnant and she was afraid. I could see in her Labrador eyes that she needed me. The weight of parenthood made me feel sick. She seemed desperate which only made things worse. This wasn't the same woman I'd proposed to. I didn't want to marry Sam anymore but now we were forever linked. I was already imagining a future full of unspoken hate and compromise. We'd have to pass our child back and forth on weekends and force conversation about the weather. I'd be made to pay child support and resent her for crippling me financially. If this wasn't the end then what was it? I'd loved her once; couldn't I fall in love with her again somehow? Why is that suddenly so unimaginable to me?

I feel self-destructive. I feel like I've jumped off a boat with cement shoes on.

I'm sinking now.

I've never felt so far away.

I've been thinking about my time as an orphan. I remember wanting a family more than anything. I remember years of neglect and loneliness because of my parents. I remember the feeling of not knowing why they left me and wishing again and again that they would come back for me. Will the vicious cycle repeat itself? It feels out of my control. I feel destined to repeat their mistakes. The idea of raising a person feels impossible. How could I raise a child when I have no idea what a happy family looks like anyway? I tried to explain it all to Sam but each time the words came out wrong.

'What's your problem anyway Ben?' she would shriek, 'How can you be so *cruel* to me?'

The truth was too hard to say out loud. *I don't want to be with you. Raise the baby by yourself. I'm not ready for this.* I couldn't say that. I had to get used to the idea that soon I would be a father whether I liked it or not.

When we inevitably stopped having sex I started masturbating on a daily basis. I would watch increasingly intense pornography and fantasise about all my exes. I thought of Lola; wondered what it would have been like to fuck Ally and yearned for two drunken girls to double-team me again. I didn't think about Sam. I didn't see her that way anymore. Why do we all want what we don't have? I'm sure if I were single I would wish for someone that wanted me for me, wanted to have my child and get married. I liked Sam when it felt like I had a choice. When I had free will I was happier.

Now I find my sneaking around has gotten steadily worse. I have started to frequent a nearby coffee shop just so I can one-sidedly flirt with a cute barista that works there. Each time she turns around my eyes drop to her rear and I imagine taking her from behind. I picture her wearing her apron and nothing else as I masturbate in the closest bathroom I can find. Where did the good times go? I am regressing into a world of fantasy because I don't like the look of my future.

The man staring back at me in the mirror feels more like a stranger. My brown hair has becoming unruly and there are more lines on my face than I remember. I force a smile but it doesn't seem to suit my face. It's like I'm an imposter.

I feel much older than I look.

As time goes on Sam's eating for two has become a convenient excuse to indulge. The fridge is regularly emptied as the days of pre-packaged meals make way for the era of fast food and sugar. The growing child she houses combines with her hefty frame to make her lethargic and uninterested. She regularly falls asleep on the sofa. Sam has never been less attractive to me and she knows it. She seems to embrace it. Sam looks at me in a challenging way that says 'You *don't* love me do you?' I'd never realised it until now but my entire relationship with Sam was built on our sex life. Without it we are slowly dying.

When we reached the third trimester I was losing my mind. Without Doug to confide in I realised I needed an escape from my routine. On a whim one afternoon I got in my car and went out to *Secrets*. I hadn't been to the brothel in years and to my surprise the exterior was almost exactly the same. I found it comforting to park in the same spot I had parked in years ago with Doug. In my wallet I had been setting aside money for weeks. For a long time my sexual fantasies had featured *Secrets*. I had already imagined fucking everyone working inside in countless perverted ways. I imagined an orgy of pleasure. I'd wondered how it would make me feel and whether it would finally be out of my system – like a teenager forced to smoke cigarettes until he is sick and never wanting to smoke again. Could I get this feeling out of me? I sat in the car park for an hour watching the closed door. When I finally made the decision and got out I found out the brothel was closed on Tuesdays. I'd never even considered what day it was. They all feel the same lately.

One night I try to sweet talk Sam but find myself giving up. I can't even convince myself to *try* anymore. What's the point? I've become depressed. Instead of calling Nathan and talking to him, like I'm supposed to, I decide to medicate myself with drink. When I have a particularly rough day and butt heads with my boss Vladimir I have no trouble justifying it to myself. No one needs to know. I don't need any more judgement in my life. I'm miserable and I know this will help me for now. Sam is in her own world and I easily hide my drinking from her. She has started blogging about her pregnancy with her new pregnant friends, which results in spending most nights on the computer. I think she knows our baby's gender too.

I wonder what else we're hiding from one another. As my drink intake increased it was more difficult to hide the effects of the alcohol. I started going to bed earlier and earlier, often on the sofa when Sam wasn't there, which only made the space between us grow.

When Sam finally went into labour I was regrettably tipsy but still got her to the hospital in one piece. The entire birth was like a fever dream. Sam zoned me out early on and the midwife did most of the support work. I had hours to myself in that room. I pleaded internally but I couldn't make myself feel anything. It felt like a nightmare. I had given up trying with Sam; I'd given up my sobriety and was preparing myself to give up on this child before it had even been born.

When the moment arrived I was numb.

'One more push Sam, come on!' said the midwife as she stared into the business end of my fiancée. I used to find such comfort from Sam. Now I'm staring at the clock.

I was completely sober as my son's first screams rang in my ears. The midwife checked him and when she was satisfied she plopped him onto Sam's chest. As he fed from her breasts I noticed her nipples had changed. In the months since I'd last seen them they had expanded and darkened. They now served their intended purpose as a food source and I knew I would never look at them with lust again.

'I want to call him Jack,' she said as tears welled in her eyes.

The midwife smiled and told her it was a lovely name.

'Is that okay, Ben?'

I nodded with indifference. Why does Sam care what I think?

Jack.

The name sounded appropriate to me. In retrospect it seemed amazing that we'd never bothered to talk about names together before now. Sam must have decided on Jack one night while blogging. I held my newborn son while Sam tried to birth the placenta.

I looked at his milk drunk little face and felt nothing. When the placenta ruptured a gush of blood left Sam and sprayed across both of our faces. I wiped Jack's face first before dealing with my own.

The newest and most innocent person in the world had just been born and I could only think about myself.

My life is over.

I have responsibilities now.

It all feels so temporary.

The walls inside *Secrets* are differing shades of purple. I still don't know how Doug convinced me to come to a brothel with him tonight but as he owns the car I suppose it's ultimately his decision. We drove forty minutes out of our way so we wouldn't run into anyone we knew from University. I guess this kind of thing is still frowned upon in modern society. Having stayed inside the lines for twenty-one years I've never been into a brothel. Two rotund women are chatting loudly at the reception desk about types of cake. I can't tell if they're prostitutes, as I've only seen prostitutes in films, but I hope they aren't. The least attractive one rings a buzzer without acknowledging us and before we know it a group of women file into the room in a scattered manner. The room fills with perfume and I notice the wallpaper is uneven in places. Imperfect.

Doug is a heavy-set computer programming student with rich parents. He tells me he's done this before so I try to play it cool.

'See anything you like Ben?' he asks with a grin.

Doug is the kind of guy that can't talk to women in the real world, so this makes sense for him. This is a transaction. I like to think I'm not as socially awkward but according to Doug my weakness is that I'm guilty of romanticising sex. I put out an intense vibe that women pick up on. That's what it's like when you're looking for the *one*. I'll be honest; I want to find the love of my life and get married. Not every twenty one year old man will admit that. Every woman you meet is potentially the love of your life, the mother of your kids and the one you'll grow old with. You're only looking until you find them. Then it's the happily ever after part of the story.

Maybe it's my virginity that's putting women off. Nobody wants to deflower a virgin these days. It's not sexy. Doug smacks his lips together like he's seen a delicious meal placed before him. His greasy fringe falls over his eyes and he brushes it away again. The women before us are in various states of undress; each outfit has been chosen to cater to a different fantasy.

Maid. Teacher. Nurse.

What's my fantasy? I look at their faces but not a single one is even trying to meet my gaze. They have the generic and forgettable looks of models on fashion runways when the focus should be on their clothes. They stare into the distance. I guess I'm supposed to be looking at their bodies but I keep wishing that they would look into my eyes. A wave of anxiety washes over me and I watch Doug for cues. He starts talking to a girl dressed in leather but he's keeping his voice down so I can't hear him.

What is he's asking her? What does he want her to do?

A blonde girl with very red lipstick finally breaks tradition and looks at me. She seems about my age and I suddenly worry that she's from our University. This woman is absolutely stunning. She's in a tight white dress that reveals her shoulders but hides her cleavage. Her long legs have just become the highlight of my night. I decide that if she went to our University I would certainly remember her.

Doug and I were at a bar on campus when he suggested this to me. I think the combination of beer and weed was just right for me to say yes.

'C'mon Benny! This is what you *need* right now. I'll be right there with you.'

'Not right *there* though right?' I chuckle. 'I don't know if I can do it with your face looking at me the whole time.'

'Aw geez, this face?' Doug says sipping his beer. 'You don't want to see *this* face when you have sex for the first time?'

Doug pulled a series of increasingly sexual faces and gave me his assurances that he wouldn't be in the room. Now that I'm faced with the reality of paying for sex I'm having second thoughts.

The girls are mostly Caucasian, but there are two Asian girls in the corner. Doug seems to have selected the girl in leather. She's definitely wearing a red wig and has wrinkles forming on her face. She touches his oversized belt buckle a few times and I can tell he's hooked. This simple flirtation seems to say *choose me and I will touch more than just your belt buckle.* Who knows how many belt buckles she's touched over the years though.

'You all good?' he asks me with that shit-eating grin of his. He strokes his chin hair.

'Yeah man, go ahead,' I say as reassuringly as I can.

Doug vanishes and it's my turn to choose. I scan the room but no one stands out like the blonde does. She looks kind of bored which makes me want to impress her. I start to wonder if there is something wrong with her. How did a nice girl like her end up in a place like this? Maybe she has some horrible disfigurement under that dress. The two large women sense my trepidation and the larger of the two makes her way around the desk and over to me. She smells strongly of cigarettes and I feel suddenly queasy. Upon closer inspection I'm now sure that neither of these two could ever convince a man to pay them for sex.

'Your friend is upstairs?' she asks through a thick accent that I can't place.

'Yes,' I manage.

'Are you going to pick a girl too?'

She smiles and I notice a mole above her lip with several hairs sticking out. I look over at the blonde as she slouches into a chair and starts texting.

'No, I'm just waiting for him.'

Chicken shit.

'Go wait outside then,' she says while a piece of snot threatens to jump from her nose.

I start to back away and become disorientated. I forget about the incline at the entrance and nearly fall over. Luckily the blonde doesn't see me stumble. Before I can be accused of staring I head outside and catch an intoxicating breath of night air. Doug won't be too long. He has the station wagon keys so I have no choice but to wait. I could just *tell* him I had sex with one of the girls and that I'm not a virgin anymore. That was the whole reason for the trip. I'm a terrible liar though. Doug will want details that I won't be able to share. He'll see right through me.

I travel down the stairs and lean against a wall opposite our car. The battered old food truck parked on the nearby asphalt has had a fresh coat of graffiti. The brothel is in a largely industrial suburb that is off the beaten path. No one has come here tonight by accident. The rock music from the strip club on the ground floor mingles with the techno soundtrack from the brothel above. I rub my hands together for warmth. Stupidly I left my jacket inside the locked car and it's almost midnight. As I'm watching my breath twirl away into the night a side door opens and the blonde steps outside. She's only about fifty metres from me and clocks me right away. I watch her light a cigarette and lean against the brick wall with one leg slightly raised. She is definitely aware of me but she's not staring. Her foot starts to track a figure eight in the dirt. Her white dress dances dangerously off the ground. It looks like she's posing for a photo shoot.

I should say hello. We made eye contact so she'll know me. She looks so intimidating that I feel the nervous urge to shift my weight. Would she talk to a customer outside though? I didn't actually go through with anything so technically I'm not a customer. Does she know that? I start to edge myself in her direction under the guise that I'm kicking a rock. It's not a strong move but I don't have a ton of game so it's all I can think to do. If I can just get close to her without scaring her off then we will talk.

If we talk then maybe we'll fall in love.

My thoughts are abandoned when the side door opens again and a huge biker steps out. His black jacket has badges on the shoulders and looks worn from years of membership. He has a cigarette in his mouth and as he nudges the blonde for her lighter I start to back away. Maybe that's her boyfriend. He looks like he could snap her like a twig.

Where the hell is Doug? I must look like an idiot loitering here. I should have taken the car keys off him. Why didn't I just pick a girl? Then I would be inside one of the warm rooms -inside one of the warm girls – instead of out here in the cold. I could go back in and act like I changed my mind. Why couldn't I just *do* it? Sex shouldn't be this big a deal. Sex does not equal love. I can't seem to get my head around fucking someone just because I feel horny. I think that's why I've started drinking. If I meet a girl and I'm inebriated maybe it will just happen. I've been overthinking this for years. I've had many targets but I just can't seem to pull the trigger.

I look up at the blonde again and everything has changed. The biker has her pressed against the wall. She's uncomfortable but she doesn't scream. He is being aggressive and blowing cigarette smoke in her eyes. With her knees bent her dress is now touching the ground. He puts his hand on her face and squeezes her cheeks, forcing her mouth into a pucker. I start walking towards them in slow motion. I don't know what I'm going to say but I have an overwhelming sensation that I have to help her.

She's a damsel in distress.

She needs me.

The blonde sees me walking over and puts her hand up so that only I can see it, pleading with me to stop. I obey and freeze on the spot. There is fear forming in her eyes now. He says something that I can't quite hear and goes back inside the strip club through the side door.

'Are you alright?' I manage to ask when I find the courage to go over to her.

She nods as she rubs her face.

'Yeah, don't worry about him,' she says with a half-smile. 'He wouldn't hurt a fly.'

I could never have beaten him in a fight. Honestly I don't know what I would have said if she hadn't stopped me. She brushes some ash and dirt off her almost white dress, shivers and folds her arms.

'Are you done for the night?' she asks.

'I didn't really…I… I'm just here with a friend,' I reply.

She shrugs with indifference and I quickly change the subject.

'Who was that guy anyway?' I ask.

'Some arsehole.'

She doesn't want to talk about it. He probably *is* her boyfriend and that was a classic lovers tiff. I notice she's wearing a necklace with a heart shaped locket on it. There's probably a picture of the two of them in there. Or maybe it's a picture of her kid. I'm finding more and more that if they don't have boyfriends they always have baggage. I don't know when everyone else found time to have sex let alone kids. It's like everyone went away and grew up and now I reek of desperation. I'm some pariah that no one wants to go near.

'I'm glad you're okay. I'll leave you alone,' I say as I start to turn.

'Have I seen you here before?'

She wants to talk to me.

'No, I'm not from around here.'

'What's your name?'

'Ben.'

'I'm Lola.'

That *must* be a fake name. Or at least a stage name. Why didn't *I* use a fake name?

'Why don't you wait inside? It's cold out here tonight.'

'They won't let me wait upstairs at reception for my friend.'

Lola nods and looks me up and down.

'Come into the strip club with me. I'm sure he won't be long.'

Doug and I never went into the strip club. I wonder what it's like in there. That would have made more sense as an appetiser. It's a perfect business model really; they get you turned on downstairs and then finish you off upstairs. Three thoughts solidify in my mind:

1. Doug probably won't leave without me.
2. Lola's hot.
3. It's fucking cold out here.

'Sure, what's the cover charge?' I ask nonchalantly.

'Nothing, I'll get you in.'

I get a great chance to look at Lola's butt as she takes my hand and leads me through the side door. It takes all the self-control I have not to try and grab it. I can feel myself getting hard against my jeans. I don't know whether it's because I'm checking out her arse or because a beautiful woman is holding my hand.

I try and think rationally.

I try to sleep on it but I can't.

It's early in the morning when I sneak out of bed. Sam is snoring and baby Jack is sleeping next to her. I dress in the spare room without showering and leave. I watch the sunrise as I drive my work van through empty streets. I have spent most of the night thinking about Lola and imagining her being shot. I imagine her death over and over again and I feel tears well up in my eyes. I blink them away and try to focus.

Old Jack has poisoned my mind with a single thought: If time travel is possible then maybe I can save Lola.

This is crazy.

Time travel.

It sounds absolutely insane to me but I can't shake the feeling that Old Jack has the answer. If his story is somehow true and he is my son then what else will he share about the future? I'm nervous to know how it will end with Sam. Was I a good father? What does Jack know about me that I don't yet know about myself? The air is crisp and I'm happy to be alone.   I find it reassuring how little I feel for Sam now. That painting has stirred something in me that I'd forgotten.

I arrive to find Old Jack standing outside with his eyes closed. It's so strange to see this man who allegedly shares my DNA standing here in front of me. It's hard to see the resemblance through the wrinkles and grey hair. But he seems to know all about me. When I park the car he looks at me and smiles.

'Have you been… waiting for me?' I ask not knowing whether I sound insane.

He gives me a reassuring smile.

'Just enjoying the sunrise.'

We head up an elevator and through to his room in silence. It is the most opulent and decadent hotel room I have ever seen. Everything seems to be made of gold. I sit on the arm of one of the many plush sofas and wait for him to speak first.

'So you heard about Lola then? I'm sorry Ben.'

'How did you even know about Lola?'

'You told me,' he replies.

I know that I didn't. At least I'm pretty sure I didn't. Why would I?

'I don't remember telling you,' I say as I fold my arms.

'Time travel is complicated. Each time I go back it erases the future. I remember things that others don't. I exist outside of time as you remember it.'

'Can you go back and save Lola?' I blurt out desperately.

'No.'

I feel myself clenching my fists as I respond.

'Why not?'

'I cannot travel back beyond my own birth.'

'And you… my son…were just born,' I say trying to wrap my head around this new reality.

'That's right.'

He sits at the edge of the bed and folds one leg on top of the other.

'You told me you had chosen me… not Sam… to give the time travel device to. Why wouldn't you choose to give it to your own mother?'

'Are you starting to believe me now?' he asks with a raised eyebrow.

'Just answer the question. Why me and not Sam?'

Old Jack gets up, starts pacing and stops at the window.

'Sam…my mother… your fiancée… she has a tumour in her brain. She will pass away in eleven months. In my lifetime I never knew her so I was always going to give the device to you.'

'She dies? Sam *dies*?'

I felt ashamed that this was something I'd sometimes wished for.

'Yes. I watched it happen. It's horrible for you but very quick for her.'

'Show me. I want you take me there. To the moment Sam dies.'

'I can't do that. The device will only go *backwards* through time. I can never go back to the future unless I do so in real time,' he says.

'This is *ludicrous*! How can I believe anything you say?'

'I don't know. I've never been able to convince you Dad.'

'Don't call me that. I'm not your Dad,' I say.

'As you wish.'

Old Jack leans against the wall and watches me as I try to process everything he's saying.

'So if you can only go backwards through time and you can't go back past your own birth, then what are you doing here?'

'As I said at the bar, I'm here to end my existence. If I give you the device and you travel back past the point of my conception then I will cease to exist. I wish I could tell you why this is happening but the truth is I'm not really sure. Ben, somewhere down the line, way in the future, one

of our ancestors invented this. He or she went back as far as they could –
to their own birth. That's as far as they could go. This device has been
calibrated to us. For whatever reason it can only be used by people that are
related by *our* genetic code. It has been passed back through the
generations of our bloodline and I'm here to give it to you. There might
have once been a reason for all of it but it's like Chinese whispers across
generations. The message has been lost. I don't know why time travel was
invented in the first place. None of our ancestors exist anymore. At least
not yet. When you go back you exist *outside* of time.'

'So you want me to go back and erase you? You'll be dead?'

'Not *dead,* exactly, but I will be gone. This version of me will
vanish. It will be painless – as though I was never born because I won't
have been born yet. I know it is hard to understand but I have lived a full
existence and I'm ready.'

'Show it to me. Where is this time travel machine?' I demand as I
look around the room.

'Alright.'

Old Jack holds up his gloved hand.

'This glove is the time travel device,' Old Jack says evenly.

'The glove?'

'Yes.'

The glove looks like the kind of glove you might wear while riding a
mountain bike. It has a Velcro strap around the wrist and is plain black in
colour.

This is impossible.

'Would you like to know how it works?' Old Jack asks with a smile.

I nod.

'Press your thumb and pinkie fingers together to activate the menu,' he says quickly.

I hold my breath and watch as the glove lights up with specks of light all over. In the palm of his hand a globe of holographic light appears. It floats above the palm of the glove and I can see little numbers on it.

'Remember this glove will only work when it is worn by someone who shares our DNA. I don't know why but that's the only way it works. It recharges itself as long as you don't take it off. If you *do* take it off… you'll start to age rapidly. I'm telling you now that you don't want that. You'll *die* if you take it off. You won't want to take it off until you've reached the beginning. You'll know when you've had enough, trust me. When you have, you need to go back and give the glove to your mother or father.'

'I don't know my mother or father. I was orphaned.'

'You will find them when you need to. And then you can decide which one of them to give the glove to. Until then, you can do anything you want. '

'But it only travels backwards?'

'Yes. And each time it takes you back earlier and earlier. When you go back you erase the future so that only one glove ever exists at a time. It's a failsafe to avoid…complications.'

My head is spinning. This is a lot to take in.

'What else can it do?' I ask.

Old Jack touches his thumb and pinkie fingers together again and the hologram globe disappears. He holds the glove in front of his face and considers the question for a moment before answering.

'I don't know everything about it. I was told there used to be some features… like instructions… but one of my grandparents found a way to disable them so I really don't know.'

'You don't expect me to believe that this glove is really a time machine, do you?'

Standing this close to him I now see that Old Jack looks world-weary. He smiles and gives a kind of half shrug.

'I didn't believe it either at first. But that was a long time ago.'

He holds out his hand and activates the glove again. He turns the dials on the holographic globe so I can see them.

'This is minutes, hours, days, years. See these numbers?' he asks.

He indicates to the numbers on the cube.

'Whenever you go back it sends a kind of pulse. As I said you'd automatically go back further each time by at least a minute. That's the default. If you don't set the timer then you go back one minute before the last time you pulsed back. You will be the only man outside of time until you travel back to your birth and give the glove to one of your parents.'

'I don't know if... I *want* to see my parents.'

'When you're ready you might feel differently about them. And you'll have adventures beyond anything you could imagine. It's an amazing ride.'

Then, without hesitation, the man claiming to be from the future snaps the Velcro open and removes the glove. It seems to power down automatically. His hand looks pale but otherwise normal.

'Now give me your hand.'

I'm on autopilot as I hold out my hand. Old Jack pulls the glove down to my wrist and straps it on tightly. He seems to strain after the simple movement.

'Touch your thumb to your pinkie finger,' he commands.

I obey.

The light from the hologram ball activates once again when my thumb and pinkie are touched together. A surreal feeling washes over me and I look into Old Jack's eyes.

'It's been amazing to meet you Dad,' he says quietly.

'I told you not to-' I start to say but I'm interrupted.

He's different now. His eyes seem to be sinking back into his head. He's looking suddenly skeletal as if he's transforming into a corpse before my eyes. Old Jack slaps his hand into the holographic globe and crushes it again my palm. For a split second we are touching hands and then he's gone. The room is the same but I'm alone again. I can still feel the sensation of his palm on mine but only for a moment.

I think I just travelled through time.

My AA sponsor Nathan owns and runs a café called *The Drop*. It's a hole in the wall several streets off the main road that coffee connoisseurs favour. The walls on either side of the door are coated by graffiti. Every time I come here the graffiti seems to change, although a trace of the old can still be seen behind the new. Nathan has a shaved head and a comically long red-brown beard that he ties up with rubber bands at three different points. He would resemble a Viking warrior if he weren't so short and stocky. I give him a wave and sit at a small table while he serves a woman holding her dog.

I haven't felt like drinking alcohol in a while but I've found that checking in with Nathan makes me feel like more in control. I've made a point of dropping in to see him every week for the last year. It started at one of those clichéd AA meetings from the movies. White plastic cups next to a water cooler and packets of plain biscuits next to tea and coffee. When I first went to AA I was in denial. I'd never hurt anyone or been caught drink driving. I didn't think I had a problem with alcohol specifically. I'd run out of money and I didn't really have anyone to talk to about it. I was failing my criminology degree and I was feeling like I was out of options. Nathan was at that first meeting and he took an interest in me. He told me later that I looked like the weight of the world was on my shoulders.

Nathan sits down opposite me and we shake hands. He takes the role of sponsor very seriously and always makes every meeting a very professional one. I think he would do a roll call and take weekly minutes if I let him.

'How have you been this week Ben?'

'Pretty good thanks. How's business?' I ask.

He flashes me a satisfied grin.

'Mate, it's been a dream. I love it. You want a coffee?'

'No thanks,' I say. Nathan waves away an employee that was looming behind me.

The music in *The Drop* is always at such a low volume that you have to strain to hear it. I can't make out what the song is but it sounds familiar.

'So, how's the sobriety going?' Nathan asks with interest.

If I fall off the wagon and start drinking again it would reflect poorly on both of us. Nathan has sponsored two other alcoholics with continued success. I don't want to disappoint him.

'Still sober.'

He smiles with his usual relief and gives my shoulder a pat. The fact that he's proud of me always makes me feel like I'm doing the right thing. This routine has become reassuring for me.

'That's great Ben, really good.'

'Thanks.'

'And how's Sam?'

'Sam is doing well. Her orders are starting to pick up so she's keeping busy.'

Nathan nods. I shift in my seat.

'An old friend of mine has been in touch actually. This guy I used to know…Doug Treborn…he wants to catch up with me.'

'Was Doug your friend during the time you were drinking?'

'Yes. We used to drink and smoke pot together,' I say with a nod.

He furrows his eyebrows. I wonder when the last time Nathan smoked weed was.

'I see. And are you afraid that if you see him again that you'll feel like drinking?'

'Um…not really… I mean… I've been around people that are drinking before. I haven't felt like drinking then so I should be fine,' I say.

Nathan strokes his beard as I speak. It's a nervous habit he has. It takes him a moment to respond as he assesses the coffee shop for customers. He's not needed yet though as the only customer is a man buying a cinnamon scroll.

'I guess the only danger is that seeing someone from *that* period in your life might bring up some of your memories from those days.'

'So you think it's a bad idea?' I ask.

I had been on the fence about this and if Nathan thinks it might be bad for my sobriety then that's probably reason enough not to go.

'I couldn't really say. Lana always tells me I've evolved past the point of making poor decisions. I guess if you don't think Doug will impact your progress then that's okay.'

Lana is Nathan's girlfriend as well as his personal saviour. Lana was the one who was there at Nathan's lowest point. He used to play in a band and when they toured he became a different person. Nathan used to go from playing guitar to drinking and partying until it was time to play the next gig. He told me he was just keeping up with the other guys from the band at first but before too long he was the instigator and didn't need companions to justify the opening of a bottle. Eventually, as these things go, his drinking affected his playing and the band didn't want him around anymore. Without the band Nathan became lost and started gambling. He met Lana while he was spiralling down and she helped him to stop. She showed him that he could be a better and happier person. I've always felt like Nathan and Lana are a more grown up version of Sam and I.

'Lana's usually right,' I say. 'She's a good egg.'

'She is!' Nathan says with a chuckle. 'I think you've evolved too. Through the program you've seen the damage that addiction has had on you… on your university degree, on your friendships. But Doug knows about your past, right?'

'Doug went to Uni with me. He and I stopped hanging out because I got out of control.'

'Oh man. I'm sorry to hear that. So maybe now that you're a little older and wiser you two can be friends again?'

'Maybe. We used to be really close.'

Doug was my best friend and simply by acknowledging that I'm starting to realise I miss him. Aside from Sam I'd say Nathan is the closest thing to a friend I've got these days, and he treats me as more of a project than a mate.

'Maybe you should spend less time looking at the past and try to look ahead Ben. Maybe there is a future where the two of you are friends again.'

'Ok. I'll meet up with him,' I say.

'That's good man. I think it will be good for you. And if you feel tempted to drink you can always call me.'

'I will.'

Four patrons walk into *The Drop* and Nathan gives me another pat, stands up and goes back to work. It was a brief catch up but it was enough.

I open up Facebook and reply to Doug.

Sounds great. I'd love to see you.

Lola examines her face in the mirror as I drive. Maybe it's not as bad as I first thought. The houses fly past in a blur as I hurry forward through amber traffic lights. I try to look cool and in control but I feel like a gazelle sliding on ice. I've never been to this suburb before and I nearly roll right over a roundabout. Lola smiles at some unspoken joke and avoids my gaze. It's getting late and I'm glad there aren't too many cars on the road. My phone vibrates in my pocket and I know instinctively that it's Doug.

I imagine he's sorry.

Also could I come back and get him?

Not this time.

I'm busy on my own adventure.

And you're a dickhead.

Without warning blue and red lights flood the car.

A police car pulls me over for a random breathalyser. I'm sober but it still causes a rush of adrenaline throughout my body. The tall dark haired officer sees Lola and suddenly I'm a suspect in a domestic violence case. He clicks a torch on and lights up the fresh bruises on her face.

'Are you alright ma'am?' he asks while his eyes dart between us.

'Da. Yes thanks,' Lola says in her Russian accent.

'What happened to your face there?'

His hand sits gingerly on his gun.

'I ran into a doorframe earlier. It's nothing. My boyfriend is just driving me home.'

I'm her boyfriend.

I don't hate the way that sounds at all. Even though it's a complete lie.

Look at me! I'm lying to a police officer with my silence.

I wish he'd stop looking at me.

'Alright then. Drive safely. And maybe get some ice on that when you get home.'

'Thanks very much,' Lola says with a slow nod.

He takes a long time to get back into his car and I wait until he leaves before I'm ready to drive.

'It's a few streets over. Let's go *boyfriend,*' she says nudging me.

I can't stop smiling.

We get to her place and I'm surprised to find it's a house and not an apartment. I don't know what I expected. It has a brown fence that is only about thirty centimetres high running around the front yard. Anyone could easily step right over it and onto her lawn. The door is a hideously bright green and the windows have bars on them. I open her car door for her and then stand there like an idiot that doesn't know what to say next.

'Are you going to come in?' Lola asks.

I don't hesitate.

'Yes.'

Through the bright green door I see art all over the walls. Clothes are strewn over furniture and there is an air of chaos to the main living room.

'Have a seat.'

Where? There is no surface available. I move some clothes across on the sofa and sit down next to them. I try to ignore the purple bra hanging off a nearby chair.

Lola stands at a wall mirror and pulls her hair up into a ponytail. She examines her face again.

'Maybe you should take a painkiller or something. Does it hurt?' I ask.

It looked like it hurt when she got it.

'I'm alright. I have some ice in the kitchen. Do you want a drink while I'm in there?' she offers.

'Ok.'

'Water?' she asks, standing in the doorway between the living room and the kitchen.

'Do you have any beer?'

'No… aren't you driving?' she says with a hand on one hip.

'Water's fine.'

I don't want to leave but *aren't you driving* suggests that I won't be staying long.

Lola leaves the room and I flip through a nearby magazine. It's in Russian. She brings me back a glass of water and I drink it nervously.

'So do you speak Russian?' I enquire after a few sips from my drink.

'Da.'

'So you're Russian then?'

'Yes. My mother and brother are still there. My father died when I was young.'

'Oh I'm sorry.'

She sits down on the sofa and takes the magazine from me. I can't place her perfume but I like it.

'It was a long time ago.'

She pauses and puts the magazine down on the floor. Lola looks me in the eyes.

'Do you want to stay here? You look kind of tired.'

I am exhausted and she must see it on my face. That's not why I want to stay though. I have been thinking about Lola for days. I want to be around her.

'I want to kiss you,' I blurt out.

And there it is. I don't know why I verbalised that thought but it's out there now, hanging thickly in the air between us.

'Do you now?'

She puts her hand on my forearm and tests the material of my jumper between her fingers.

Time for a dose of courage. Nothing ventured, nothing gained.

'Have you ever seen someone and had to meet them?' I say trying to stay relaxed.

'No.'

'I saw you that night upstairs in the brothel and I had to meet you. I knew at that moment that not meeting you would have been a big regret… maybe the biggest regret of my life.'

'A big regret huh? That's sweet I guess.'

'So can I?'

'Can you what?'

'Kiss…kiss you.'

Lola smiles at me and leans forward.

'Yeah… go on. Kiss me then.'

I don't know where this confidence has come from but it's here now so I try to use it. I move myself closer and kiss her. At first I don't know what to do with my hands and they sit motionlessly by my sides. Lola wraps her arms around me and kisses me back. It's such a shock to my system. My arms finally engage her waist.

This is actually happening.

I'm not imagining it. I feel short of breath and find I have forgotten to breathe during the kiss. I gasp for air as I break our lips apart.

'You're a nice guy huh?'

'Yeah. You're a nice girl right?'

'Well, I do strip for money.'

'That's kind of nice. There are a lot of lonely people out there.'

'You sound like you know something about it…'

'Yeah. I get lonely sometimes,' I say.

'Me too.'

I look around the room.

'Maybe you should get a cat. For company.'

Lola laughs.

'I'm not home often enough to feed a cat. Besides, I'm not looking for a commitment like that.'

'You want one of those neighbourhood cats that comes over and says hi, has some food and goes home to his real family. You get to give it a quick belly scratch without having cat hair everywhere.'

'I'm more of a dog person,' Lola says.

'Cool. I like dogs.'

I've never had a dog or been associated with any dogs in my life but it feels like the right thing to say. She rests her hand on the back of my neck.

'So I hear you are still a virgin Ben.'

As I suspected the girls all talk. It's only natural. I'll never be able to show my face at the brothel again.

'I am. Unfortunately.'

'So are you saving yourself for marriage?'

'No.'

That's not the first time I've been asked that question.

'Then what are you waiting for?'

'The right girl.'

Lola smiles at me. She's so happy with my response that she leans in and kisses me again.

Wow.

'Get some sleep. I'll see you in the morning.'

I swallow away everything I want to say next. I must exercise self-control.

'Okay.'

I move the remaining debris, lie down on the sofa and find it's amazingly comfortable. I look at my phone and find Doug has given up on reaching me. Lola leaves the room and vanishes into a bedroom. She is intoxicating to be around. I could kiss her all night. I consider going around the corner and bursting into her bedroom. Before I can chicken out Lola comes back and drops a blanket in my lap.

'I'll see you later,' she says turning on her heel.

'Goodnight Lola.'

I stare at one of the paintings on the wall. It's a tiger with a dead peacock in its jaws. There is a pool of blood that has formed around the corpse but all the blood is green. The tiger's teeth have been stained green too. Its eyes are a fiery red.

It's been years since we've spoken but today I find a Facebook friend request from Doug. What does he want? There is no message attached but we are approaching his birthday. Maybe he's just feeling nostalgic? I turn my phone off and roll over. Sam is asleep, of course. She's almost never woken up before me in the six years we have been together. I hop out of bed, shower and head back into the bedroom naked. I look at myself in our full-length mirror and suck in my gut a little. I'm definitely fatter but not by too much. I still look good naked, Sam tells me all the time. She usually sleeps with her hands under her face. I think about the time I proposed last year and how there was an awkward phase where every morning she would have the indent of a diamond on her cheek. I thought it was so funny. I consider climbing back into bed with her and waking her with affection. The thought is short lived though as I have to get ready for work.

My uniform consists of a long sleeved t-shirt and overalls. Plumbers are always associated with 'plumber's crack' so my boss Vladimir solved it forever by making us wear brown overalls. While being a plumber is a valid occupation, and one that keeps money coming in, it's not what I thought I would be doing. When you're young you can do anything. Over the years you learn all the things you're not good enough at or things that don't interest you. I never wanted to be Prime Minister or go to space. I wanted to be a policeman. I wanted to catch bad guys. I remember signing up for criminology and thinking it sounded like I was training to be Batman or something. After I discovered girls I was less interested in that world though.

I remember someone at University spread the rumour that I had slept with a stripper and some girls responded to it. Suddenly they were interested in me. I had sex and I was good at it! All the girls told me I had a huge dick and then afterwards they told their friends I had a huge dick. The word about me got around without any effort on my part. Everyone wanted to try me out and see if it was true. I was one of the cool kids for the first time in my life. I stopped spending time with Doug, but I kept using drugs.

Weed. Ecstasy. Cocaine.

I used to have some bad habits. I was an addict in my youth. It started with all that female attention. I often think about the time I had a threesome. I like to remember my sexual conquests when I'm with Sam and things are feeling kind of repetitive. It doesn't mean I don't love her but I find if I focus on some key moments my muscle memory will do the rest.

Women were my sole focus back then. I hung out at that University bar long after I dropped out of my degree. Maybe I was trying to recreate that night. I never came close to such a visceral experience again. I never saw the girls from that threesome again either. They knew where I lived so I guess they didn't feel as good about the experience in the light of day. I had no right to keep hitting on students but I kept on doing it. I was numb but I wasn't mature enough to realise how meaningless it was.

Sam was the first genuine connection for a long time. She didn't have sex with me right away, which meant something to me. She wasn't disposable. She had value. Sam and I met long after my failed foray into criminology. She and I met after I stopped drinking and womanising.

She met me at the best possible time.

Sam runs an independent catering company that mostly makes healthy meals for childcare facilities and retirement homes. Every day our kitchen looks like an assembly line. Sam makes the meals in the afternoon or early evening and then everything gets vacuum-sealed and sent out. They don't cater breakfast. I guess it's easy to make kids or old people eat fruit or cereal. The workload allows her a relaxed lifestyle and she has lots of time to read. Lately I've noticed she's been reading about parenting.

She wants kids more than anything. I like to remind her that if we have kids they might not let her sleep in like I do.

One of Sam's latest endeavours is to rearrange our place. She's been nesting since I gave her the engagement ring. The living room was painted over the weekend and as I pack one of her healthy meals for my lunch I step back and take in the new colour. The purple walls are reminiscent of a brothel from long ago. It's not a colour I would have chosen but Sam seems really taken with it so I try to focus on the present instead of the past and just go with it.

It's pretty sad that Doug and I lost touch. We used to do everything together. I use the fact that he has requested my friendship as an excuse to stalk through his profile on Facebook. I look at the pictures first. He looks thinner and younger without facial hair. When we were friends he was always stoned and unshaven, now he appears to be healthy. There are pictures of Doug in mountain climbing gear. Last year after some prompting from Sam to read more I browsed a book about climbing Mt Everest and decided that mountain climbing wasn't for me. All Doug's travel pictures are cheesy touristy ones with well-known landmarks. It's hard to miss the cute little blonde in his pictures either.

I head upstairs and find Sam is finally awake.

'You're up then?'

'Sure am handsome,' she replies.

I love that the first words she says every day are complimentary. We kiss and she playfully tugs at my overalls.

'Do you have to go to work right now?'

'Yeah, Vladimir has me booked solid.'

I don't like Vladimir and that has little to do with the fact that he is my boss. He's condescending and doesn't know the first thing about plumbing. His father owned the plumbing business and he inherited it along with his many other investments.

'Do you want to try and have lunch together?' Sam asks hopefully, full of beans like a Labrador as she tries to make plans with me.

'I won't be local but I took one of your pre-made meals.'

'Good, that's what they're in there for.'

Sam tries to fix her brown hair into a ponytail with a nearby hair tie. It's curly and seems to have a life of its own. She's so beautiful.

'My friend Doug from University sent me a Facebook friend request.'

I can't keep anything from Sam. For some reason she has this look that makes me want to tell her *almost* everything.

'Oh yeah? What was he studying?'

'He was into computers. Computer programming and software design. That kind of thing.'

'You were good friends weren't you? I'm sure you've mentioned him before.'

'Yeah the best,' I reply thinking back to our trips to strip clubs and weed inspired shenanigans.

'So why aren't you friends anymore?'

'I dunno. I think we just drifted apart you know?'

'Did you accept his request?' she asks.

'Not yet.'

'Why?'

'It's been almost a decade. I think we are different people now.'

I'm not the man I used to be.

'Well, if he's the one reaching out what's the harm? He probably just wants to say hi.'

'I don't know. It's such a long time ago. I don't know if I want to dredge up the past. I want to leave it behind me. I don't really want to think about how I dropped out of Uni. I mean… I was friends with Doug before I really knew who I was.'

Sam tilts her head to one side.

'And who are you Ben?' she asks dramatically.

'I'm just a plumber who's running late.'

I give Sam a kiss and start to leave.

'Love you!' she yells out as I leave the bedroom.

'Love you too baby!' I yell back.

I get in my van and go from job to job doing what I do best.

At lunchtime I add Doug as a friend and by the end of the workday he's sent me a message.

Hey Ben! Can we meet up? It's been too long! Doug.

My van isn't where I parked it.

I head home in a taxi that I have reception call for me.

I feel disorientated.

Is this real?

Old Jack has sent me back one year if I believe the settings on my new glove.

According to him he no longer exists. He's tricked me. I wonder if it was as painless as he thought it would be. In the back of the taxi I continue to examine the glove. I click the holographic setting back to be only one minute. I don't want to accidently go back another year.

I need to see Sam.

I need to know if this is real or not.

The taxi drops me off across the road from my house just in time for me to see myself. It's me from one year ago. I'm getting into the driver's seat of my plumbing van and leaving for work in my brown overalls. It's such a bizarre sensation to watch yourself from afar.

Yet there I am.

This is beyond an out of body experience.

This is something else entirely.

Ben from one year ago looks happy as he turns on the radio and drives right past my taxi. I cower in the back seat like prey avoiding an apex predator.

He doesn't see me. The taxi driver doesn't notice my other self and leaves me at the kerb.

I walk with haste to the door. My head is clear now but the sensation of déjà vu is intense.

I knock.

Sam opens the door and looks at me with surprise.

'What are you doing honey?' she says as she starts to smile. 'Did you forget your keys?'

She looks younger and more care free. I'd forgotten how amazing her body looked before she got pregnant.

'Are you real?' I say while putting my hand out to touch her face.

'What are you on about? Why have you changed clothes?' she asks looking confused. 'Are you coming in or what?'

Sam pokes her head out of the doorway and notices the empty driveway.

'Where's the van?'

I start to panic. I don't know how to explain any of this to her. I touch my pinkie and thumb together creating the holographic orb again. She is awestruck and silent for a moment.

'I...'

I don't know what to say.

So I won't say a word.

Sam stares unblinkingly as I crush the orb with my bare hand into the palm of the glove in the same way Old Jack had done.

I had it set for one minute but I must be back a bit earlier than that. I'm standing facing the closed door. As I turn to scan the front yard I see the van still parked behind me.

Ben from one year ago hasn't left for work yet. I've travelled back to at least one minute before my *last* journey. Is that what Old Jack had said? There can never be two of me running around so it always takes me back to one minute before by default. This is getting confusing. His tutorial on how to time travel seemed all too brief. The taxi ride over took about twenty minutes so my past self will be leaving the house around then.

I peer into the window and watch the younger version of myself getting ready to leave. He runs a comb through his brown hair. I run and hide in my neighbour's bushes and wait. This is really happening. I look at my gloved right hand in astonishment. The déjà vu continues as I watch myself leave in the van again some minutes later. He moves in exactly the same way. The same song plays on the radio.

I knock on the door for the second time.

'What are you doing honey? Did you forget your keys?' Sam asks in the same inflection.

'I forgot to tell you how beautiful you are,' I reply and swiftly kiss her.

Sam is taken aback but matches my intensity right away. We stumble into the house and continue kissing. It is so clean inside compared to the home I have been living in. That messy future of ours is still in the distance.

'Where do you want to go?' she asks between kisses.

I motion to the floor in the middle of the living room and she obliges without words. Sam slides off her pants and underwear before lying down on the rug. I drop to my knees initially but then slide myself into a push up position and start going down on her. It's so spontaneous and fun. I feel like I'm cheating on the Sam from my time but technically she doesn't exist anymore. Also this Sam is definitely cheating on the Ben from this time but she doesn't know there are two of us. It all combines in my head to make it even hotter. I try to think back but I can't remember any occasion when I came home again this soon after leaving for work. I don't think we'll be caught but if I'm wrong I'll use the glove to escape.

I continue to swirl my tongue around rhythmically much to Sam's delight. She grabs my head so I can't get away. She's going to come. I reach one hand up and invade her bra. I gently twist and flick her nipple and I can feel she's close. I unclip my belt and pull down my pants. With my dick in my hand I crawl up and slide myself easily into Sam. She starts to bite her lip and I start to thrust. She teeters on the edge of climax for only a moment. During that time I study her face knowing that this will be the last time I will ever fuck her. I'm sad that this is the end but I would rather it end now before we make each other miserable. Just like Old Jack this version of Sam will cease to exist. She won't remember any of this the next time I pulse back through time anyway. I'm the only one that will know this moment ever happened.

When it's over she collapses onto the rug and I withdraw myself.

'Oh my *God*.'

Sam isn't religious so I'll have to take this as the ultimate compliment.

'You're going to be late for work,' she manages to say as she kicks me playfully.

'I'm not going to go to work anymore,' I say with a smile.

'Uh…okay wise guy. How are you going to get money? Win the lotto?'

'I haven't decided yet. Maybe that's a good idea.'

She bursts out laughing which makes me smile. I'll miss Sam. It's sad knowing that she has a brain tumour that will eventually kill her. If I stick to Old Jack's plan and go back all the way to my parents then neither of us will be here and none of this matters anyway. Sam will never have to die again. I have to learn to detach myself. Sam, just like everyone else in this world, exists because I haven't been back to give the glove to my mother or father yet.

They are temporary. I can do anything I want between now and my birth.

I give Sam a kiss goodbye.

'Get to work,' she says as she goes to clean herself up. 'Vladimir will be pissed.'

'Love you Sam.'

'Love you Ben.'

I walk out of the house and down the street. I know that I could continue my life in this time but there is already a version of me here to do that. I can be anyone I want to be. I'll change my name. I'll get a lot of money just like Old Jack had and do whatever I feel like. This glove is a blessing and I'm a God.

I sit nearby and listen to every line they say. On a small pocket-sized notebook I write down their exchange.

'Is this seat taken?' Doug asks with one hand on the chair opposite Jessica.

I still can't believe how different he looks.

'No, please,' she motions for him to sit down.

'Thanks.'

He compliments her beauty and asks what she's reading.

'Great Expectations,' she says with a smile.

There is a bookshop a few streets over and I make a mental note to grab a copy. It's been a few years since I read it last. Doug vaguely remembers it from University and quotes enough to keep the conversation going. He awkwardly asks if she's waiting for someone and she shakes her head. She's smitten.

I try to remember back to when Jessica and Doug told this story at dinner. It's definitely love at first sight. Even though I can tell he's nervous I've never seen Doug look at a woman this way before. He fidgets, putting his hands into and then out of his pockets. Jessica looks radiant as she sips an iced tea. She can't stop running her hands through her hair. She blushes when he finds an excuse for some light physical contact. He gets her number and says he has 'great expectations' about their future together. It's corny as hell but it makes her smile.

I walk straight to the bookshop and get a copy of the book. I read it twice while sitting in luke warm baths in my hotel. I memorise my transcript of their meeting. I no longer want to follow Doug.

Now I want to spend some time with Jessica. When I feel ready I pulse back to a little before their meeting and wait.

I wait patiently for the time to go by before this can all unfold again. I've had to fill the hours with films and hobbies. Sometimes it feels tedious but I try to use the time to read about history and think about places I might like to time travel back to.

Safe places.

Familiar places.

Like a child waiting for Christmas morning I'm impatient at times but when the day comes I am ready to change history.

When Doug gets close to the coffee shop I call him. He and Ben haven't spoken in years at this point in time but his number has never changed.

'Doug is that you?' I say knowing it is. My ability to act has improved.

'Yes. Who is this sorry?'

'It's me. It's Ben.'

I watch him stop in his tracks.

'Ben? Oh my God it's been forever.'

You have no idea.

'I wanted to call you and say sorry. I'm going to kill myself today.'

So very abrupt of me.

'What? That's not funny Ben. Are you being serious?'

'Yes. I wanted to make amends before I went. I'm sorry about everything.'

A pause. I watch Doug pace the street while his mind processes this new information as fast as he can.

'Where are you right now?' he pleads.

'I'm at University actually. I'm going to jump off the library. Maybe they will put up a plaque or something.'

'Don't…look…will you wait for me? I'll meet you inside the library okay? Don't do anything until I get there. Promise me?'

He's sincere. It's strange but I'm glad I know he's truly my friend. This feels like such an odd test to prove said friendship but nevertheless. Time travel makes for many strange situations.

'Ok. See you in a bit,' I say a little too calmly.

I chose the library because it was near enough that I trusted Doug would hurry over. I'm going to steal their moment and make their first meeting *our* first meeting.

Ben and Jess.

I like the idea of that.

I watch Jessica get herself a drink. After a breath I repeat Doug's actions.

'Is this seat taken?' I ask with the same inflection as Doug used.

'No, please,' she motions for me to sit down.

'Thanks.'

I sit and I ask her what she's reading. She shows me the cover of her book. That's odd. She said the name out loud for Doug. I decide to adlib a bit and hold up my own copy of *Great Expectations*.

'What the Dickens!' I joke.

She gives me a slightly uncomfortable look and closes her book.

'Did you just buy that you stalker?'

'No, I just happened to be reading it. It's good isn't it?' I offer with a practiced smile.

I just happened to be reading this incredibly old book.

'You should probably go. My boyfriend is coming to meet me.'

For a moment I think she means Doug. For so long I have associated them together. But she doesn't mean Doug – this would have been the first time they ever met.

She doesn't mean anyone.

She just doesn't want to keep talking to me.

I've fucked it up. I walk away and turn a corner into an alley. I look at my notes and realise I didn't compliment her. I pulse back and get ready to do it all again.

The time that I must wait passes more slowly this time. I concentrate on my first impression. I exercise and buy new clothes.

'Is this seat taken?' I ask again.

'No, please,' she says as I sit down eagerly. My heart beats faster in my chest.

'Thanks. Wow. You are *beautiful*.'

'Thank you. I'm Jess.'

'I'm Brad.'

'Ah… my ex-boyfriend's name was Brad.'

'Was it? That's annoying.'

I try to salvage the situation but I can feel it slipping away like a ship being dragged to the bottom of the ocean.

Reset.

'Doug I'm going to kill myself.'

…

'Is this seat taken?'

…

'Thanks. Wow. You are stunning. I'm Brad.'

'Ah… my ex-boyfriend's name was Brad.'

'Really? Looks like you have a type.'

Jessica gives me a disgusted look.

…

Reset.

'Doug I'm going to kill myself.'

…

'Is this seat taken?'

…

'You're a creep.'

…

'Thanks. Wow. You are stunning by the way. I'm Bobby.'

Steve. Luke. Leroy. Dean. John. Johnny. Pete. Phil. Mikey. Nate.

I try it so many ways.

…

'Get away from me *loser*.'

…

'Look, you seem nice but...'

…

I start to feel bad about pretending to commit suicide. I tell Doug I need him to pick me up, drive me to the airport and bail me out of jail. A few times I just intercept Doug and catch up.

I try to mimic his stance and his voice. I try every tactic I can think of to seduce Jessica Nash.

Nothing works.

With each pulse I'm trying to find the perfect name and be the perfect guy. She reacts differently than she did with Doug. I start to realise that she must have genuinely liked the look of him. There was chemistry there that she doesn't have with me. I'm exhausting myself. Each time I repeat the same tired pick-up lines and attempt to make Jessica fall in love with me I get further away from the genuine meet-cute this should have been. My delivery of the lines becomes indifferent. I am literally just going through the motions.

I didn't care how I did it – just that the end result meant *I* got Jessica and Doug didn't.

But it never eventuated because I'm not Doug.

I'm me.

It isn't real anyway. I'm sick of this moment. I'm sick of trying so hard and not getting anywhere.

I get a nice hotel room and don't come out for a week.

When I emerge I decide to find my past self and voyeuristically watch him. I see a man without concern for the future. I was lighter on my feet back then. I seem happy. I'm meeting new women all the time. I stalk myself from bushes and cars. My past self isn't a full on alcoholic yet but is definitely binge drinking to excess. I watch from windows as he fucks one-night stands. I remember most sexual encounters fondly. Some have been lost in time. One night while watching I see young Ben with a radiant brunette outside the Uni Bar. She's wearing a small tight top highlighting her cleavage. What's she doing with me? Surely she could have found someone better. They've both been drinking and they decide to call a taxi.

I don't remember her at all. My younger self stumbles recklessly towards the road and crosses it without looking.

He's so lucky not to be hit by a car!

The brunette giggles and clicks her heels a few steps behind. They get into a taxi and drive away into the night.

How could I not remember her? She's gorgeous and I have no memory of our night together. I have to know more. I pulse back and wait. It takes weeks before time catches up to that night again. This is the worst and most tedious part of time travel.

I drug the taxi driver. I steal his taxi with the sole purpose of picking them up. I create a mock disguise but I'm assuming since I don't remember her I wouldn't remember a taxi ride. I tell myself that this is worth finding out as I lay low and wait for the moment to come. When it finally arrives I'm positioned in the taxi at the front of the line, ready to pick up young Ben and the brunette. They stumble into my car and Ben yells an address at me.

'26 Booker Street.'

I have a vague idea where that is. I start to drive while I listen to them talk. I learn that her name is Nellie. Ben tries to have sex with Nellie in the backseat of my taxi. It's one of the more surreal experiences of my life. Nellie is into it too. She lets Ben take her breast out and put it in his mouth. I keep trying not to look but it's an impossible task. She has an amazing body and I feel like an absolute pervert. It's a straight road so I keep on driving. Neither of my passengers is wearing a seatbelt anymore. I wonder how much the original taxi driver let happen in his car. I tilt the rear view mirror down and see Nellie stick her hand into the front of her pants. She is moaning softly as she touches herself. Ben keeps licking her left breast while fondling the right one. It is like I'm not even here.

I start to become aroused.

I can't help it.

I've never seen myself from this angle. I've never seen this girl. It's an entirely new experience that I completely blocked out.

Why don't I remember this?

When I get to the red light at the end of the street it happens.

'Now!' she yells and they both get out of the car in unison. Before I can speak they are running away and I'm left gobsmacked. I watch the thrill seekers run into the distance but make no attempt to catch them. What would I say if I did?

When I have finished crying and my head stops spinning I stand up.
I look at Helena one final time and walk away. I don't want to remember
her this way.

I won't.

I can smell her perfume for only a moment before it starts to rain.
Some people in the street see me walking away from her dead body and
start to whisper to themselves. I'm disappointed that they didn't appear
when I was being shot at but it doesn't matter now. Nothing matters here
and now. Someone has called the police and I can hear a siren growing
ever closer. My pace remains steady as I walk to the park. I have to stay in
nice open areas. I don't want to appear inside a wall when I pulse back.

I settle myself down on a wooden bench and play with the settings
on the glove. When three armed police surround me I realise I haven't
been afraid of consequences in years. I could have been shot and died in
the street with Helena. Maybe that would have been better than feeling like
my heart has been ripped from my body. The policeman closest to me
starts yelling and I stare at him in wonder. This man has a real job and a
real life. His family must love him and probably worry about him every
day.

I want a life.

I want things to go back to normal. I smile at him and as I clap my
hands together he's gone.

I find a quiet hotel room and sleep my dark thoughts away. I remind
myself that she's not *really* dead. She's alive again now that I'm back
here. I have to clean myself up and focus on the rest of our lives.

On the future.

I head back to Helena's place and knock on the door. She opens it in a purple robe that she clutches closed with one hand.

'Yes?' she says with a beautifully confused look on her face.

It's so good to see her – even though she has no idea who I am. In my head I repeat my mantra.

I will not let her die. I will not let her die. I will not let her die.

'Hi I'm Brad and I'm new to the area. I just wanted to meet some of the neighbours and say hello.'

'Hi Brad. Nice to meet you.'

'And you are?' I ask while trying to remain non-threatening.

'Helena.'

'That's a beautiful name.'

'Thank you.'

'Wow. This has been great. I hope to see you again soon,' I say as I smile and walk away.

She's alive.

I just had to see her for myself.

This is how it should be. Boy meets girl and they fall in love. Time travel is not a requirement. I want it to be real. I use my notebook of lottery numbers and sports results to win a lot of money. I financially persuade the owners of the place next to Helena to move out and I move myself in. It takes less time than expected. I start creating a garden in my front yard as an excuse to see Helena as often as possible. She heads out for regular excursions and each time has a conversation with me. I try my best to be charming, loveable and the man of her dreams. I start to notice our conversations getting longer and better. They don't end; they merely pause until the next time we speak. Every night I exercise so that I can be attractive to her as well as protect her. I smile at the thought that she found me handsome once and use it to motivate myself. I meditate often and think about the notion of happiness. I know in my heart that Helena is the only person that I've ever truly been happy with.

And then I have a moment of clarity.

I promise myself that I'll never use the glove again.

I hate that I can't take it off. We are stuck together until the day I die. But I am not bound by it and I do not have to use it. I can have a normal life with Helena.

Helena eventually becomes curious and asks about the glove. I tell her Old Jack's lie about being burnt in a fire. The lie proves a clever one and she doesn't ask any more questions. Slowly Helena starts flirting with me. We are building something here. Sometimes I think she can see right through me. Maybe she can tell I'm in love with her already.

'Brad do you want to come in and have dinner with me tonight?' she asks one morning out of the blue.

My heart beats faster.

'I would love to.'

'Are you a vegetarian or anything?' she asks.

'I'll eat anything. I'm easy.'

I think back on my time as a vegetarian and smile. I missed meat too much to keep it going. We set a time and she goes on one of her walks. I resist my old instincts to follow her. To watch over her. I tell myself that she'll be fine. The day she dies is still deep in the future. I spend the rest of the afternoon grooming myself and worrying about what to wear. I have butterflies in my stomach for the first time in a long time. I'm excited and hopeful. I feel like everything is new again and my life with Helena is full of possibilities.

No more time travel.

I have a life to live here. No more excuses. Dinnertime finally arrives and with wine in hand I make the twelve-step journey from my place to hers. She opens the door in a flowing green sundress and I hold my breath.

'Hi Brad. You look nice.'

I have chosen a chocolate brown coloured shirt and dark jeans for the most important meal of my life.

'You look incredible,' I offer as I finally exhale.

We open the wine and talk about Helena's Russian heritage. She tells me about her childhood and her dream to come to Australia. She opens up about her work and her friends.

Helena and I talk until the early hours of the morning when my face hurts from smiling. She quantifies this as the best first date she's ever had. I remember trying to perfect my date with Jessica. Helena and I got it right the first time. We kiss at the door and I feel myself blush. It's like a dream come true. Everything is just right for the first time in a very long time.

As the weeks go by we are in contact every day. We talk about life and our hopes for the future. Helena finds excuses to hold my hand or hug me. It is in these moments that I realise how wonderful intimacy can be. I've been lonely without her.

We talk about books we've read and ones we are yet to read. I've spent so much of my downtime watching films and reading books that I have to hold back during these moments. I'm cautious about revealing my knowledge of the future. I note her recommendations and read them when I'm alone at night. We discuss art and music. With each piece of art I feel like I'm learning another secret about her. Every time I'm in her home I see the painting of the tiger with the peacock and each time I feel a wave of nostalgia wash over me. It feels good to be living day to day like this. I sleep well at night and eat three meals a day. I'm happier than I can ever remember being. Somewhere out there another version of me is living my past life and trying to catch up.

I'm ahead for once.

I try to forget it all and be present with the love of my life.

She shows me pictures of herself as a girl.

'I was so fat,' she says with disgust. She just looks like a normal kid to me.

'You look healthy now,' I offer.

This seems to be the right response. When she asks to see pictures from my past I panic and tell her they were lost in a fire.

'Is that the same one that burnt your hand?'

I nod and tell Helena that I don't really feel like talking about it. I don't want to lie but there will always be some topics that are off limits.

She seems to understand.

When Helena speaks I listen so intently that she says she feels like I'm looking into her soul. I think back on the moment I watched her die. I felt her soul leave her body and when I look at her now I'm so happy she's alive that it makes me want to cry.

I did it.

I saved her.

For now at least.

Everything that happens to Helena from now on will be because of the glove. Sometimes I worry that I'm forcing her to love me. I've been bending the universe to match the way I want it to be. Other times I'm sure it's destiny.

As the moment of her death comes ever closer I talk Helena into a career change. I tell her that she is the most talented artist I have ever seen and that her work should be in a gallery. It takes some convincing but eventually I build her confidence up to the point where she agrees to show her work. When the time comes I pay hundreds of people to attend her show and buy most of her art under an alias. I have it moved to a storage unit.

Helena is amazed with her instant success and that night is the first time we have sex. It is familiar to me and comforting to us both. Helena tells me she is falling in love with me. I tell her I'm falling in love with her too.

We buy art supplies and set up a studio space for her to work. I lie in a hammock and watch her paint until she tells me I'm distracting her. She paints me, which I find flattering, although I hardly recognise myself sometimes. Helena sees me as a confident and happy man. I must have become this without ever realising it. I estimate my age to be almost forty but I don't feel that old. Does time travel affect appearance? Helena asks me about my parents and I tell her they died when I was very young. I tell her I don't really remember them. That night while I meditate I wonder whether they did die. They certainly never came looking for me after they left me at the orphanage. I wonder whether I'll ever want to go back and find out more about them. At this moment going back in time again is the furthest thing from my mind. When I look at Helena in the summer sun I feel like this is all that matters.

The present is a gift.

I'll have to take Helena out of Australia soon. In order to guarantee she doesn't die I need to remove her from harm's way. I want Helena to travel with me and experience the world so I formulate a plan. Using my knowledge of upcoming lottery results I take Helena out one night and we buy a lotto ticket together.

'If we win the lotto we should jump on a plane and see the world,' I say as I hold the ticket.

'I would like to go back to Russia and see my family.'

'And we should get married and have a fancy wedding,' I blurt out without meaning to.

Helena smiles and says 'Sure, *if* we win the lottery.'

We have a quiet dinner at her place and fall asleep without checking the results. Helena is sitting on top of me when I wake the next morning and she's holding the ticket in her hand.

'I need to tell you that I wanted to run. I thought about leaving you here and running away but I couldn't do it.'

'What are you talking about?' I say knowing all too well.

'You came into my life and changed everything. I'm so grateful. I love you Brad.'

'I love you too. What's going on?' I ask.

'We won the lottery!' she says, beaming.

We embrace and I do my best to act surprised.

'Why aren't you more excited?' she squeals bouncing the mattress around me.

I tell her that I'm in shock but the truth is I have probably won the lottery hundreds of times now.

'So…will you marry me then?' I ask with a grin.

'YES!'

They say that having children will change you and that is definitely true. It feels like the toothpaste is out of the tube and I can't get it back in. Sam and I will be staying at the hospital for a least a week while she and Jack recover. I told Vladimir that I could come back to work before that but he insisted I spend this 'magical' time with my family. It's boring at the hospital. The bland off-white walls and overpriced food make me feel like an inmate. Nurses and midwives fawned over Jack. Sam's mother calls every day demanding new baby pictures to show off to her friends. She promises to visit as soon as she had organised someone to water her garden.

It feels as though Sam has to feed Jack fifty times a day, which leaves me flipping through television channels mindlessly. Everything melds together after a while. Sam and I speak from time to time but always about inconsequential matters – never about anything serious. She's waiting for me to break up with her. She wants to be the victim.

I leave the hospital as often as I can with any excuse that comes to my mind. I have been out for food, changes of clothes and most importantly alcohol. There is a bar just down the road and across the street, which I have been frequenting on a daily basis. The money I had intended to spend at *Secrets* has been used for dozens of glasses of whisky, which I have pretended is in honour of my son but in fact is because of him.

His birth spells my eventual death.

This must have been how my parents felt when I was born.

No wonder they gave me up.

'Mind if I sit with you?'

I look up from my booth to find an old man of about seventy standing over me with two glasses of alcohol. His hair has receded to reveal a field of wrinkles and blemishes on his forehead. It's not unusual for me to chat with some random bar flies but I'm impressed that this one has had the foresight to buy me a drink.

'Is that for me?' I ask motioning to his second glass. He nods and I happily take the glass from him as he sits down.

'Thank you,' I say as I finish the whiskey quickly in a satisfying gulp.

I notice he is wearing a black glove on one hand. It's a plastic looking bicycle glove with a Velcro strap at the wrist. I find it odd that he is only wearing one.

'What's with the glove?' I inquire bluntly.

'Piqued your interest has it? Well… I was involved in a fire that left parts of my body… damaged.'

'I'm sorry,' I say. 'That sounds horrible.'

'It was a long time ago. I find the glove makes people less uncomfortable than my burnt hand does.'

'Fair enough,' I say while swishing the leftover ice in my glass.

He shifts in his wooden chair but I refuse to offer him my plush leather corner booth. He'll survive.

'This bar is a bit of a shithole,' I say as I scratch my neck.

'Why are you here then?'

'My girlfriend just had a baby at the hospital across the road.'

I've now verbally downgraded our relationship status from engaged to just dating. This guy doesn't need to know my life story.

'Congratulations!'

'Thanks. I'll tell her you said that.'

'Sorry to pry but it is *your* baby too right?'

'Yep.'

'Then why aren't you more excited?' he asks.

'I guess it just doesn't feel real yet,' I lie. I've held my son and it's all too real.

The old man insists on buying me a few more drinks. I don't want to go back to Sam yet and she probably doesn't care if I'm there or not so I take him up on the offer. I'm pleased to find out that the old timer is pretty flush with cash and seems to share my love of top shelf drinks. After an hour or so I'm feeling much better.

'This has been so much fun man,' I slur.

'For me as well.'

'I never asked you why you were in hospital. Was someone looking at your burns or something?'

'No, I wasn't in the hospital,' he says looking a little confused.

'Oh yeah... we didn't meet in the hospital we met in the bar didn't we?'

Now I sound confused.

'I came here to see my father.'

'He's still *alive*? He must be like a hundred years old!' I laugh while trying not to spill my latest drink.

'He's alive alright,' the old man says putting down his glass. His face is still and he seems to stare through me as he speaks. 'You're my father Ben.'

'Huh?'

'You are my father. I'm Jack. I'm your son.'

'My son is four days old.'

'I know. This is going to sound mad but I can travel through time. I am your son and I've travelled back here to meet you.'

His words seem to suck all of the oxygen out of the room.

…

I don't know how to respond. The alcohol makes it even worse.

This man is clearly insane. I never told him my name was Ben or that my son is named Jack but that doesn't prove anything.

Did I say something?

Maybe I did say our names and I just can't remember because I've been drinking.

'What do you want from me?'

'I came here to end my existence and give you my time travel device.'

I can't help but laugh.

'Oh yeah? Is it a Delorean?'

'It's back at my hotel room. I'd like you to come with me.'

I'm not going to follow this crazy old man back to his hotel room.

He stands up and looks around the bar. I notice that with the exception of the bartender we're alone. I push off the table and stand as well. The whisky makes me dizzy but I manage to stay upright.

'Listen, I don't know who you are but you're not a time traveller.'

'I am.'

'You're not.'

He smiles.

'You're probably a boring old man that's looking for a reason to get out of bed in the morning.'

'I am Jack Hawkins. I'm your son whether you believe me or not.'

Hawkins?

'Ha! My last name isn't Hawkins. It's Stanley.'

'My mother's last name was Hawkins.'

Sam's last name *is* Hawkins.

Shit.

This is a very specific fact for this stranger to guess.

'Ok, well then come and say hello to your Mum. Let's go back to the hospital together and have a family reunion.'

'I have chosen to give the ability to travel through time to you, not her.'

'What? What are you…' I trail off. Now the room is starting to spin.

'I know this is a lot to take in but it's all true.'

'I don't believe it,' I slur again in a drunken haze.

'I know you don't. It's such an impossible thing that I'm saying and I know that. This is the ninth time I have had this conversation with you. There seems to be nothing I can say to make you believe me right now.'

I study his face for a moment.

'Okay... good. I'm going to leave.'

I start to walk away and he stops me with a gentle hand on the shoulder.

'Will you take my card? I've written the name of the hotel I'm staying at on there.'

'Sure, fine. Whatever.'

If that's what it takes to walk away from this conversation.

I take the business card and put it in my pocket.

'I think you'll want to come and see me when you hear about Lola.'

I wake to find Lola perched on top of me. She's wearing underwear and a t-shirt. Her small frame feels fragile and light. I sit up and my eyes are drawn to her nipples pressing out against the fabric.

'What are you doing?' I manage to ask in my half-awake state.

'I want to make love to you.'

She kisses me, prying my mouth open with her tongue.

I kiss her back.

'Wow. You have bad breath,' she says jokingly.

It must be early in the morning but there is no clock in the room. I don't feel like I've slept much.

'Here,' she says seemingly producing a glass of water from thin air, 'drink this.'

I drink the water in big gulps. As I do Lola strokes at the hairs on my chest and I feel myself getting turned on.

'Do you want to make love to me too?'

I nod.

This is it.

It's going to happen now.

Finally!

I feel my face flush as my mind starts racing.

She takes the empty glass from me.

'I'm kind of nervous,' I admit.

'You're going to be great. Let's just kiss to start.'

Lola and I kiss again. I reach out and touch her breasts through her t-shirt. She stops me and smiles.

'There's plenty of time for that.'

'I want you.'

I want to take off her clothes and feel our bodies fit together.

She throws her arms around my neck and gives me a hug. It would be a tender moment if I weren't so aroused.

'I like you Ben.'

'I like you too.'

'Listen…'

She runs her lips across my earlobes as she moves to face me. I silently pray she isn't going to ask me to leave.

'Ben, I know you're looking for the right girl. I don't think I'm her.'

Shit.

She doesn't want this after all.

'I'm trouble,' she says quietly.

My mind flashes back to the man in the jacket hitting her outside *Secrets*.

'What trouble are you in?'

'It's *my* trouble not yours. You don't need to know,' says Lola.

'I need this. I want… love.'

Damn. What a stupid thing to say. There is obviously a lack of blood getting to my head.

'I don't love you. You may feel like you love me but this is not love.'

Lola thinks I'm saying I love her. I've confused her. Time to be upfront again.

'Can we… have sex?'

'Yes, if you like. I would like that also.'

I look at her face. It's kind and soft. Lola smiles at me again.

'I hoped you would say that,' I say as I lean in and kiss her.

She's amazing.

'I know this is your first time but I need to tell you something,' she says as she tucks her blonde hair behind her ear.

'Yeah?'

'We can have sex more than once tonight. We can have sex as many times as you like.'

I laugh. Her confidence in me is very funny.

'Okay…' I say.

Lola grinds very lightly against my dick. She seems pleased.

'I had some Viagra from one of the girls at work and I crushed it up and put it in your water.'

This renders me speechless.

Has it hit me already?

'Don't be angry with me.'

'I…'

I'm not angry. I'm actually strangely impressed. She sourced Viagra from some girl at work, which means it probably wasn't intended for me initially. Some guy has missed out on the night I'm about to have. She didn't know this was going to happen tonight. I had no idea this was going to happen.

It's actually kind of perfect.

I was worrying that I wouldn't last and that I would disappoint Lola. I've been worried about every aspect of sex and anxious each time I've come close to having it. Here I am with a woman that *wants* to have sex with me. She wants to have sex as many times as I want and she doesn't want this to turn into love. Lola has somehow turned me into a stud.

'That's great. Thank you,' I say.

Lola lifts her t-shirt over her head and my hands instinctively grab at her breasts.

I'm finally going to have sex. She moves to undo my jeans and I'm more than happy to help her. She uses her hands to free me and takes a long time examining my penis. Lola looks like she is concentrating, taking a mental snapshot.

'You have a big cock,' she says without meeting my gaze.

'Thank you.'

Lola climbs back onto my lap.

'Have you ever thought about doing porn?'

'Ha… no.'

'I'm not really an exhibitionist.'

'After tonight when you are more comfortable with sex you should think about it. The world should share your gift.'

I don't know how to respond. I don't want to say the wrong thing and jeopardise this so I reach out to take off Lola's underwear. An impossible task while she's straddling me. She stops me and stands up. Lola slides her underwear down, bending her body to a ninety-degree angle. When she straightens herself my eyes wander. She's so gorgeous. I remove my jumper and t-shirt in one motion. We're both naked except for the socks on my feet. She senses my desire for her and straddles me again.

My penis seems to search for her as we kiss. I feel her hand expertly guide me to the right spot. She takes me inside her and I feel every inch.

'Do you have a condom?' I ask, a little too late.

'We don't need one.'

I go against my instinct and decide to keep going. My hands ricochet from her perfect butt to her perfect breasts. She feels amazing. Lola clenches herself around me and my mind goes blank. I come inside her. My eyes force themselves shut and I cannot open then for several minutes. She caresses me and my whole body shivers with sensation.

We have sex again and again that night. I find out everything I like and I'm surprised to discover some things I don't like as well. Lola is a great partner. I'm happy. I tell myself this was the right time.

Lola was right.

It feels like love but I know it's not. Eventually we stop and everything feels different. I find sleep easily and feel carefree for the first time in a very long time.

'Wake up.'

Lola.

She gives me a playful shove and I'm awake. The Viagra has worn off and I'm still completely exhausted. It all feels like a wonderful dream.

'Time to go Ben.'

She is dressed in casual clothes that almost match mine. As I get dressed I look around at the room in the light of day. The tiger painting is haunting. It stands out as the oddest thing in an otherwise normal room. I wonder if Lola likes tigers. I wonder who painted it. She offers me a cup of coffee and I decline. I can see she's in a rush.

'I really had a great time,' I offer, hoping to see more of the Lola from the night before.

'Yeah it was fun,' she responds while packing up a handbag.

Should I ask if we could do this again? I really do want to. Flashes from last night are seared into my mind.

Lola under me, Lola above me, Lola and I as one.

She came last night. I couldn't believe it at first but she assured me it was real. I'm brimming with confidence now thanks to Lola and her little blue pill.

We head out the door and Lola gives me a quick hug.

'Have a good day,' she says as she heads toward a waiting taxi.

'I could give you a lift?'

'Don't worry about me. Bye Ben!' she calls out as she gets in the back.

'Bye.'

What a rushed ending!

Lola and I shared something that I'll never forget. I get in my car, which is really Doug's car. I wonder if he got home all right. It's probably a bit early to call. He probably had sex with Rachel. No sense in wasting something he had already paid for.

I drive home in silence thinking about Lola.

I can't even believe that happened.

I can't wipe the smile from my face.

I decide I want to fuck the most famous woman on the planet. I want to infiltrate her world and then make her fall in love with me. The woman I have set my sights on is Simone McIntyre. She is the highest paid actress in Hollywood and in anticipation I have leased a million dollar estate in Beverly Hills. I research her backstory and learn everything I can about her. I read her favourite books and watch all her films. I study her until there is nothing from the public record that I don't know. Simone is a strikingly tall woman with mousy brown hair. There are no pictures of her with any other hair colour so I assume she is a natural brunette. Her body of work starts in the independent scene with bit parts. Some of the films are hard to find and she has very little screen time. She is effortlessly gorgeous in all her films but people remember her best as *Angel.*

In *Angel* she played a woman that became the most famous model in the world. Male viewers were treated to an almost naked Simone McIntyre on screen, which tripled her fan base overnight. Life imitated art as the world clamoured for Simone in the same way the paparazzi did in the film for her character Angel. She appeared on magazine covers and was hounded wherever she went. Simone was nominated for every award under the sun but failed to win any. Over the years she was dumped by several famous men leading people to fall in love with her even more. She was a victim. She was fascinating and I couldn't wait to meet her and add her to a growing list of female conquests.

I wondered if meeting someone so angelic and perfect would change me in any way. Would I be able to forget about Lola? Would I fall for Simone and stay in this time with her? I had spent years abroad and sometimes I thought about going back to see whether Old Jack was telling the truth. A part of me wanted to know whether Sam really died and how

'I' was coping with fatherhood. I wanted to go and see what my life was like but I was still frozen with fear. My other self and baby Jack were the only two people I knew of that shared my DNA. They were the only people in this time that could take the glove and use it to their advantage. I had been so cautious up to this point and it felt stupid and risky to check in with a version of me that wouldn't exist for long anyway.

The operation begins with my attendance at all the Hollywood parties as a man of mystery. I am suddenly *The Great Gatsby* come to life. I become an investor and donate to various film projects. Having knowledge of the future of the film industry agrees with me and I know all the right projects to finance.

Soon I become a dynamo.

I'm a man of influence.

People start listening to me. If I say a film will make money – it does. I am always right and no one else knows why. I am photographed with up and coming actresses at premieres. People started talking about Brad Dumas in the social pages. I make famous friends and learn the industry from a Producer's point of view. When I have finished laying the groundwork I'm finally ready.

It's time to meet Simone McIntyre.

The first time I see her in the flesh is at a party. The night has been arranged to loosen the purse strings of potential investors like myself in the hope that we will assist in the financing of some tacky film. It's a forgettable thriller that Simone is contractually obligated to star in. The Producers need some start up cash that will hopefully entice a studio to bankroll the film. I am dressed in the most expensive clothes I have ever owned. My velvet suit has been custom made and this silk shirt feels amazing against my chest. I'd told my new Hollywood stylist that it was a big night for me and that money was no object. As a result the watch on my left hand is more expensive than most houses. The glove on my right hand is - of course - one of a kind as well.

Simone sashays into the room with all eyes on her. A smug looking producer leads her around like a prize horse as she smiles politely. This is a well-rehearsed routine. She wears a deep cut sparkling black dress that dives past her cleavage to her belly button. It's a difficult look to pull off but Simone seems at ease with everything. Her hair has been tied into a long plait and swept to one side of her face. Simone wears little make up as she has no need for it but her lipstick tonight stands out because it is sparkling silver. We lock eyes across the room and she holds my gaze. I nod politely and shrug as if to say 'Who knows huh?' She smiles widely and I wait patiently for my turn to meet her.

It's almost eleven when I'm finally face to face with this goddess.

'Hello. I'm Simone,' she says looking fresh despite her hours of mingling.

'I'm Brad Dumas. It's a pleasure.'

'Have you decided to invest in our little film then?' she says raising one eyebrow.

'I'm certain that with you attached to star it will be the biggest film of the year.'

In truth I have no idea about the future of this film. As I've never heard of it I assume it will never see the light of day. The tagline is *There are three sides to every story* which I'm not sure even makes sense.

'You're very kind.'

'You're very beautiful,' I say quickly.

'Thank you.'

'I'm sure men tell you that every day of your life.'

'Some do,' she says maintaining her poise.

She runs her fingers across her chest and I do my best not to look down. I keep my eyes locked onto hers and she smiles as though I have passed some silent test.

'I'm not most men,' I say as I adjust my expensive watch in front of her.

'You are getting a reputation Mr. Dumas.'

I *love* that Simone just said that. I have literally spent months establishing myself in Los Angeles in the hope that she would notice me.

She has.

Simone McIntyre knows who I am.

Everything is going according to plan.

'I hope it's a… *good* reputation?'

'I wouldn't be standing here otherwise.'

'Would you like a drink?'

She waves her hand and declines.

'I don't drink.'

'Neither do I… *anymore*,' I say lying.

'Why did you quit?'

'I guess I wasn't very good at it. Or maybe I was *too* good at it.'

She smiles and seems to size me up. Perhaps she's imagining me in a drunken state.

'Why did *you* quit?' I ask.

In all my preparation for tonight I'd never read that Simone had a drinking problem.

'You can't quit what you never start.'

She's so pure. I want her even more. Famous people have a kind of orbit that draws you to them. Simone McIntyre is like no one I have ever met. She is polished and proper. I now see her as the ultimate conquest. I want to bring her down to my level. I want to dirty her up. I want to know if I can do it.

She isn't making it easy for me.

'Are you excited about the film?' I ask to keep things moving.

'I'm always excited to start a new project.'

It's the kind of line a publicist would tell her to say. I take a chequebook from my pocket.

'How much do you need?'

'The budget is twenty five million dollars. We're trying to raise half of that tonight.'

'So if I write you a cheque for twelve and a half million dollars you'll send everyone else home?'

'Yes. I suppose that would end the need for the fundraiser.'

I write the cheque and hope I can close the deal with her before anyone tries to cash it. Simone is genuinely impressed.

'You are full of surprises Brad. Thank you.'

'No problem.'

'I know that *your* support will certainly make some other investors take notice.'

'I hope they do. You are a very talented actress and I want you to have the creative freedom you need.'

Simone smiles and it feels like everyone else has vanished.

'I'll be right back,' Simone says and walks over to an associate. They return together.

'Excuse me Mr. Dumas?' says the wiry man with steel rimmed glasses.

'Yes?'

'You've single-handedly financed this film. The studio will pay for the rest. Thank you for this. Truly.'

'If this will please Miss McIntyre then I'm happy to do it.'

Simone seems to blush and covers it with a sip of water.

'You're really very generous,' she says when she finishes her drink.

'I'm a great admirer of your work.'

The man with glasses senses he is no longer needed and goes back to a group of men with suits that take turns pointing back towards me. One man gives me a thumbs up and another gives me a cheer. Twelve and a half million dollars buys you a thumbs up and a cheer. Hollywood is a messed up town.

'I'd love to visit the set and spend some more time with you Simone. Once shooting gets started.'

'I'm sure we can accommodate you.'

We flirt back and forth like professionals. As midnight approaches I start to worry that she'll disappear like Cinderella.

'Would you see me again?' I ask trying to secure another face to face.

'Are you asking me on a date?'

'That would make my night,' I say offering her my top of the line embossed business card.

'Thanks Brad. I'll be in touch.'

She never answered the question.

Simone McIntyre kisses my cheek and I place my hand on her hip. There is electricity in the air.

'Goodnight Simone.'

'Goodnight.'

I leave the party in a state of euphoria. My driver takes me home, drops me off and I'm alone again. It's all been worth it. The night is cloudless and it is as if a million tiny stars shine only for me. As I reach for my house keys I hear a familiar voice behind me.

'Brad Dumas?'

I turn and see Ben Stanley standing at my gate like a ghost from a time long ago.

'Are you Brad Dumas?' he asks again.

'I am.'

It must be two in the morning but I don't check my watch to confirm.

We look like brothers. Identical twins. We stand for a moment and size each other up. I am wearing the clothes of a richer man but physically we are almost the same.

'I'm sorry to do this to you... to drop in on you like this. I didn't know how to get in touch with you,' he says as he grips the bars of the gate. I instinctively put my gloved right hand into my pocket and slowly move towards him.

Does he know?

'Who are you?' I ask trying to keep calm.

'My name is Ben Stanley and I saw you on TV. I think you might be my brother. I was adopted and I never knew my parents.'

He isn't here for the glove.

Ben is here for me.

He's looking for family – for a connection. There is probably a lot I could learn from Ben but it's all too late. The present he's living in is about to be erased.

I've made a mistake. By creating the Hollywood Producer Brad Dumas I've put myself in the public eye. I've allowed Ben to find me and now I've blown my cover.

'I'm sorry,' I say as inexplicably I start to cry. 'I never wanted this for you.'

'What are you talking about? Do you know me? Have we met? Do you know my parents?'

He's clutching at straws. Ben is a desperate man.

'Did Sam die?' I ask.

He freezes and a look of terror comes over his face.

I don't know why I asked that and Ben clearly doesn't know what to say next. Sam must be alive although I've lost track of time. She might be pregnant with Jack as we speak.

It's irrelevant now.

I take the time travel device out of my pocket. I don't want to think about this anymore. I set the hologram and press my hands together. I watch Ben's confused face disappear and suddenly it's raining outside the Beverly Hills mansion.

The party's over and I'm alone again.

I've been dating Ally for a month and a half. I met her on campus in the hallway one day and we spoke for about a minute. Afterwards Ally became the reason to come to class early. We clicked straight away. She has short brown hair and wears a lot of checked shirts. She's sexy in a mousy, tomboy kind of way. When chatting between classes Ally mentioned some random band. I said I would be at the gig *for sure*. The band's music sucked. It felt like someone listened to *Blink 182* once and then wrote a song about it. I drank so much alcohol that dancing seemed like the only thing to do. Ally danced with me. Somehow she was impressed with my moves. When some other girls chatted to me on the dance floor I could tell it made her jealous. That's when I knew I had a chance with her.

For our first date we went to the movies. My favourite actress Simone McIntyre was starring in *The Sensation of Flying* about a woman who falls in love with a hunky pilot. The movie was formulaic and overall pretty forgettable. I thought that a romantic comedy would be a good idea but Ally has supernatural tastes. Ally likes *Buffy the Vampire Slayer* – a whole lot. She's some kind of super fan.

'Oh my God. This is simply the best show ever made. *Ever*! Joss Whedon is a God.'

I'd never seen the show before. Since then I've been forced to watch about thirty episodes. I don't mind because we make out a lot between episodes. Often to the theme music on the DVD menu screen. It's created a Pavlovian response where we get together each time we hear the song.

Ally is happy to take things slow with me. She doesn't know I'm a virgin, of course. It's too soon and I don't want to scare her off. Ally thinks women shouldn't rush into sex anyway which is perfect for my situation.

'Men and women can be friends you know. This isn't *When Harry Met Sally.*'

We both live on campus so we are in each other's rooms a lot. My University work has suffered somewhat since we started dating. When I started this semester I was getting distinctions and now I'm down to credits. I'm a little bit worried that if we do have sex I'll start failing. I don't want to stop dating her though. I feel like I'm onto a good thing.

Ally loves music and likes making playlists for us to listen to. She sits on my bed in jean shorts and asks me what I think.

'I don't know. I like it,' I say, hoping for some affection.

'What do you like about it?' she asks inquisitively.

'It makes me think about you.'

I'm not smooth.

Ally seems much smarter than me too. If I get stuck or don't know what to say I'll just try and kiss her. It's the easiest relationship I've ever had. I want to lose my virginity though. I've got to tell her. I'm hoping she'll help me and we can get through this together. I just hope I don't come off as desperate.

Doug hates her.

He thinks Ally hates him so he's pre-empting her hate with his own. I think he dislikes how I want to spend time with her. Doug wants to take me back to the brothel. All I can think about now that I'm with Ally is how unromantic it would be to have sex with a stranger. I've imagined having sex a million times. I've watched porn. I've jerked off. I know what to do. I'm very worried about being a disappointment though. I think about how quickly I came with Willow and know I'll come just as quickly with Ally. But if I can make her fall in love with me then it can just be the funny story of the first time we had sex and not become the story of the *only* time we had sex.

She arrives after class and I order us a pizza. I would order Meatlovers if it was just for me but as I'm trying to get laid I order a Vegetarian. I've been working at a bookshop on campus that sells students their course books. It's not enough cash to take her out for dinner. I have some modest savings but it's all been earmarked for my studies and my future.

'How was your day?' she asks while taking off her shoes and sitting at the foot of my bed.

'It was okay. Just working at the shop this morning and then had a lecture.'

We sound like a boring married couple.

'Did you wanna watch something?' Ally asks reaching for a *Buffy the Vampire Slayer* DVD.

We sit on my worn blue sofa and eat our pizza. We lament the struggle of being a vampire slayer that is in love with a vampire. Ally talks about what we should do on the weekend and which bands are playing at the campus bar. It's comfortable. After a time we start kissing and I can feel the blood rush from my head.

'Ally?'

'Yes Ben?'

'Do you want to… have sex with me?'

She raises her eyebrows.

'Tonight?' she asks.

'Oh… I just meant in general. Tonight? Sure… maybe,' I offer.

Just say it. She's going to find out anyway.

'I've never done it before,' I add quickly.

'What?'

'Sex.'

'We've done some stuff though,' she says.

'Yeah… but I've never gone…all the way.'

I hold my breath.

'So you're a virgin?' asks Ally.

'Yeah.'

She sits up straight. I thought she might have already assumed this was the case but she seems in total shock.

'I don't want this to sound harsh… but I don't think I should have sex with you then.'

'Why?'

'I feel like I've been getting to know you pretty well over the last month and… you're all about romance. It doesn't feel like we're compatible.'

The paused screen shows Buffy stabbing a stake through the heart of a nameless vampire.

'Ok… but I think I'm falling in love with you,' I say proudly.

'See! It's these grand gestures. You're not in love with me. You just want to have sex with me. I think you'd have sex with anyone.'

'I wouldn't have sex with anyone. In fact I *haven't* had sex with anyone. This is special. It means something to me.'

I find it genuinely offensive that she thinks that. This isn't a game to me.

'This is *nice*…sure. I like hanging out with you but it's sort of become like hanging out with a friend,' Ally says as she starts to stand.

'Have sex with me?' I plead.

I've become desperate again.

'I think you'll regret it. I was actually thinking about breaking up.'

'What? And when were you going to tell me?'

'I was going to tell you this weekend. After your birthday.'

My birthday is this Thursday.

I'll be twenty-two years old.

A twenty-two year old virgin.

I have no idea when Ally's birthday is.

Ally and I break up. I'm sad and I decide to have a few drinks. All I have tomorrow is lectures and I justify that I could miss them all without too many people noticing. When it seems like a good idea I jump in a taxi and head forty minutes out of my way hoping to see Lola. The driver talks to his friend on speakerphone for the duration of the drive and the car smells of fast food.

I get out of the taxi and I'm happy to discover the alcohol inside my system is keeping me warm from the cold night air. I try not to stumble and find my way to the doors. Someone has engraved a very vulgar word on the wooden frame. I fumble for the handle and give it a turn.

Locked.

I bang on the door a couple of times. A female voice yells from behind the door.

'What is it?'

'Are you open?' I call out.

The door opens slightly and Lola is suddenly standing in front of me wearing a robe. It's unexpected to say the least. The door is still latched and I can only see some of her face clearly.

'Not tonight, we open Thursday to Sunday.'

A flicker of recognition crosses her face.

'I remember you. Is it… Ben?'

I hope she can't tell I'm drunk. It's nice that I made an impression last time.

'Hey… Lola, right?'

'Listen we're closed tonight. If you need to you should head upstairs. They're open tonight.'

The brothel.

There's a lot I want to say to her but I'm not given the chance. A burly man unlatches the door and opens it wide, giving a view of the stage. There are about fifteen people standing around and two almost naked girls sitting casually in the middle of the room. Lights on stands are blasting them from all sides and one man is playing with the settings on a camera.

Are they making porn?

The burly man looks at me quizzically. He thinks he knows me.

'Are you...?' he starts but trails off.

'No he's not,' interrupts Lola.

He frowns and barks at me.

'Closed set.'

The door slams and I'm left alone. The night seems colder now.

They were shooting porn. What else could that have been?

If Lola is in a porno I will definitely find and watch that porno.

I head upstairs to the brothel and open the black door. I'm staring at the purple walls again, this time without Doug. I approach one of the two large receptionists leaning against her desk.

'Good evening,' I say confidently as though I come here all the time.

'Hi handsome, are you looking for some company?' she says without adjusting her stance.

'Yes.'

She begrudgingly moves herself behind the reception desk and presses some kind of silent alarm. I wait against the far wall, this time standing clear of the incline. Two men in suits laugh their way past me out the door. I try not to make eye contact with them as they go.

Women file into the room just like last time. There are fewer girls to choose from tonight. I recognise one of the Asian girls from last time but no one else stands out. I'm asked to choose and without hesitation I select her.

I need to be more decisive.

The girl smiles and beckons me to follow her. She leads me through a corridor filled with forgettable techno music. She stops at an ATM.

'Do you want to get some cash out? Otherwise it will appear on your credit card.'

I don't have a partner to hide this from and I don't care if it appears on my credit card. I withdraw three hundred dollars anyway and hope I'll have some left afterwards.

'Do you want to do it in a waterbed? It doesn't cost any extra.'

Suddenly I'm making choices. I'm invested in this. I say yes to the waterbed and no to her costumes. I want her to be naked. Who knows how often those costumes are cleaned. The only thing she makes me do is shower. Every man has to shower. Minutes later I'm standing in the shower and sobering up. I'm already aroused and although I'm tempted to masturbate I remind myself why I'm here.

To have sex.

With a stranger.

To have *unromantic* sex.

To get it over with.

With this stranger.

Fuck.

This is nerve-racking.

I enter the makeshift bedroom to find my lady of choice on the waterbed. She has changed clothes and is wearing aqua blue underwear and a see through top. Her nipples are tiny and are pressing firmly against the light material.

'What's your name?' I ask hoping for a real sounding answer.

'You can call me Michelle,' she says softly.

I head to the bed and sit down on the edge. The waterbed gently rocks me up and down and I feel ridiculous and childish for choosing it.

'What's *your* name?' Michelle asks as she places a small red pillow at my feet and kneels towards my lap.

'Ben Stanley.'

'It's nice to meet you Ben. What can I do for you today?'

It occurs to me that I don't have to *have* sex with her. Michelle's suggestive kneeling has reminded me that there are other things we can do. I'm sobering to the reality of this now and even though she's cute this is not how I imagined losing my virginity. I ask about oral sex and I'm given a price that makes me sure I couldn't afford actual sex anyway.

Oral sex it is then.

Michelle takes down my pants and boxers shorts in one motion and I raise my hips to allow her to do so. She spends a short time examining my dick for potential diseases before she starts. It's an awkward moment. I'm regretting sitting on the bed like this and I ask her to stop while I lie down. The waterbed is distracting. Looking at her is distracting too.

'You're big boy,' Michelle says slipping into broken English.

'Thank you,' I say not knowing what else to say.

She crawls up over my groin and starts. Her vice like grip holds my dick and balls together as she glides up and down. This is only the second blowjob I've ever had. I got head from a previous girlfriend but she wasn't very experienced and everything she tried hurt me. I wasn't confident enough to direct her so we never tried it again. You have to be gentle with a man's genitals. It's a sensitive area. Michelle is a pro. Literally.

It's silent except for the occasional sound of her mouth smacking or the waterbed shifting. She glides her thumb over my balls while she works. Everything feels amazing. Using two hands on me doubles my pleasure and I come. She keeps me in her mouth for a long time afterwards. I open my eyes when she finally releases me and feel a little embarrassed.

'Sorry about that.'

'It was my pleasure,' she says calmly after cleaning out her mouth.

She's a good actress to pretend for me. It must be a difficult job to do this kind of thing night after night. I decide to give her the full three hundred and she happily lets me talk to her for a while. I feel like I've paid for her silence.

'I'm a virgin and I'm having a tough time with it.'

'People are making fun of you?'

'No, I'm just overthinking it. Like, tonight with you I talked myself out actual sex and settled for a blowjob.'

'Oh you *settled* for it did you?'

'That's not what I mean. You were fantastic.'

'Thank you.'

'I just mean…'

'You're scared?' Michelle offers. She's counselling me now.

'Yeah.'

My one word response hangs in the air. The stillness of the waterbed adds to the silence. Michelle looks at me and starts to pout.

'Don't be scared. Sex doesn't hurt. It feels even better than that blowjob did.'

'I guess I just figured I would be with someone I loved when I finally had sex.'

Michelle pops some gum in her mouth and starts chewing it. She offers me a piece but I decline. She needs it more than I do.

'Don't you want to be good at sex so you can impress the girl you fall in love with?'

'I felt embarrassed when I… when I *came* just now.'

'You shouldn't. It's natural.'

'I'm just worried I'll come too soon and wind up disappointing her.'

'Well if you want to come and practice with me I'll be right here. Maybe we can have sex next time big boy.'

It's a tempting offer that I will have to sleep on.

I have to work tomorrow and it's already been a weird night. I have the monotonous pleasure of stocking shelves with thick books and standing at the door to check people's bags for potential theft. I think about Ally on the way home and decide to call her despite the constant glare of my taxi driver. She doesn't answer and I can't think of anything meaningful to leave on her voicemail.

In Russia I meet Helena's family. Her brother Oleg hugs me for a long time and expresses how happy he is that I have made an honest woman out of Helena. Her mother is just happy to have her daughter home regardless of how long we choose to stay. Apparently Helena has been absent for years. I am given a glimpse of a life I never knew. There are simple moments of a family unit having breakfast around a table and the routine of saying goodnight to those you love. It's touching to see where Helena came from and it makes me love her even more.

Helena and I buy some property near her parents and make it our base of operations. I have promised to take her on lots of holidays and give her inspiration for all the new paintings she will do in the future. We spend the major holidays in Russia with her family and I start to learn some basic phrases. At night I hold Helena and she snores quietly. She's content, which makes me content.

She's alive and we are together.

I dream about my younger self. What becomes of me if I never meet Helena? Who does Ben eventually lose his virginity to? I interrupted the natural progression of my old timeline and my old life.

Who is Ben Stanley now?

Maybe without this distraction he graduates and joins the police force. What if he gets shot and killed? The glove lets me exist outside of time so even if he dies I would think I'd be okay.

I know I will be.

My mind wanders back to the time I strangled him in anger and I remind myself how much I have evolved since then. I've changed. I'm not a violent man anymore.

Helena and I get married when her mother becomes sick. On the day we become man and wife it rains from sunrise to sunset. We pose for photos under large black umbrellas, that were the only ones available, and we kiss in front of a three-tiered chocolate cake decorated in edible fondant ribbons. That night without a word we fall asleep due to pure exhaustion and consummate the marriage in the morning.

When her mother dies a few weeks later Helena cries more than I had ever seen her cry before. She says she feels broken and when she paints now she uses only black and brown. Some days she smiles at me through tears and sometimes she sits silently. She pores over her mother's belongings and shows me an endless stream of old photographs. The sorrow that comes with losing both parents paralyses Helena for a long time. It is a dark period in our marriage and I don't know how to pull her out of it. I can't relate to her level of loss, as I never mourned my parents. I find that I don't know what to say at times and so we let our nights pass without affection. Her brother sells off the contents of their family home in an auction and Helena declines her share. I feel impotent even though I am wearing the most powerful device in existence. I contemplate using the glove to go back and undo this suffering but know that ultimately Helena's mother will still die just as Sam would always die.

Death is inevitable.

One day I will die too.

After about a month Helena tells me she wants to travel again so together we conquer Europe. We re-tread some familiar places that I never thought I would see again. Having my wife there with me enhances the experience. Under the Parisian moon she smokes cigarettes and tries to blow smoke rings. I tell her she shouldn't smoke but come off sounding like a scolding parent.

'Who cares?' she says as she leans over the balcony railing.

She's being reckless.

It's a beautiful city but I can't concentrate on anything when Helena is in danger.

'I do of course.'

'We all have to die sometime. Maybe if I die before you my art will become valuable.'

'I'd rather have you than all the money in the world.'

And it's true.

'Do you ever think about death?' she asks as she stubs out her cigarette against the metal railing.

I pause as I consider whether or not to continue telling my wife the truth.

'Every single day.'

'I think we should try and have a baby,' Helena says softly, 'I feel like my mother would have wanted me know what that feels like.'

And suddenly with this revelation I can see a pathway through her grief. If Helena has a child she will take her mother's place as the matriarch of our family. I would have the chance to experience the life I could have had with Sam.

I don't blame Old Jack for sending me back here.

I didn't love Sam anymore and I was miserable in my life as a plumber.

It seems a lifetime ago.

I think about Jack.

My only son that I never even had a chance to know. Why didn't he let me raise him and get to know him before he gave me the glove? Maybe I wasn't ready to be a father.

Maybe I'm ready now.

Helena is the right person and there will never be a more perfect time. I'm happier with Helena than I ever was with Sam.

'I'd like that. I've always wanted to be a father.'

It's a white lie. Technically the version of me that didn't want to be a father isn't me anymore. I'm Brad and I want to see where this goes. Helena wraps her arms around me and I feel tears forming in my eyes. Paris seems like the perfect backdrop for this moment.

We leave for Italy and a summer of sex and, with any luck, procreation. We rent a villa opposite an old vineyard and ride bicycles into town. One day as we eat fresh bread with olive oil at a cafe Helena tells me she wants to paint a mural on a wall while we are here. We negotiate with several shop owners, despite the language barrier, and eventually one agrees. Helena sends me away. I walk around for hours wondering what she'll paint. When I finally see her new piece I'm surprised by its simplicity. It's a rainbow made up of household items. A red kettle, a green basket, a pink door. It's not her most sophisticated work but I'm happy to see Helena is painting with colours again.

In the evenings we light candles and talk about our unborn child. Helena wants a girl that she can name after her mother.

'What would you name our son though?' I ask as I twist my wedding ring around my finger.

'Gregor?'

I make a face.

'What about Thomas?' I ask.

'Hmmm… It's hard to imagine. What about Luke?'

'No…it makes me think of Star Wars,' I say.

We keep making love in the hope that Helena will become pregnant. I'm not concerned about gender or names yet. I've been haunted by the idea that I've created a strange new future by marrying Helena.

I wonder if the moment our child is born they will come back and offer a glove to me. Will they see the glove on my hand and know I am an imposter? What happens if *two* people exist outside of time?

What if they come back to give the glove to Helena this time? If I don't go back and give the glove to one of my parents will the glove find a way to skip me using Helena? Will it course correct? Questions like this keep me up later than I'd like and I regret that I have no one to talk to about it. This is the one secret I must keep from my wife.

She can never know what I know.

Months pass and Helena doesn't fall pregnant. I finally feel ready to have a family with her and I can't. Has my sperm been damaged somehow? People don't like to stand too close to microwaves because of the idea that it could leave them impotent. I shudder to think what time travel has done to me. She starts to seem more and more distant and tells me she misses her brother Oleg so reluctantly we stop travelling and go back to base in Russia.

I feel like I've let her down.

The light at the end of the tunnel isn't any closer.

The worst part about being here is that I don't speak fluent Russian yet. Helena speaks to Oleg in whispered secrets that make me feel like an intruder. I find myself entering the room just as they stops speaking. I turn to look at Helena and she looks guilty.

I've never seen her look that way before.

Her brother Oleg now treats me as though I am a cancer that threatens to envelop his sister. I don't understand when this shift occurred.

We don't fight out loud. Our marriage now has a silent narrative just beneath the surface. I become desperate to give her a child. A child that will solve our problems and make us happy again. I find an English-speaking doctor and make an appointment to get my sperm checked. When the results arrive I learn that my sperm count is especially low.

I'm told I won't be able to impregnate Helena without some scientific intervention. The odds are ridiculous. The doctor tells me I may as well give up. There is no clear cause but I know in my heart that the years of time travel have changed my body. I'm a shadow of my former self.

I don't want to tell Helena.

I don't want her to leave me.

I've spent so long building this dream that I don't want it to come crashing down around me.

I'm scared.

Helena changes her painting style again and all I can see in her artwork is reproductive organs. Each image is surrounded by what looks like a womb. Art is all my wife can birth. We've stopped talking about children altogether. We have sex once a week and because I'm so excited and the occasion is so infrequent I never last long enough to satisfy her. She doesn't want me for anything other than my sperm these days. I find comfort in the order of day-to-day life. I have few possessions to maintain but since I am the more domestic of the two of us I tend to clean the house methodically. I find myself cleaning up after Helena a lot but I don't mind. I clean and organise her painting supplies and regularly restock her inventory.

I mind that she doesn't seem to notice.

She seems like she's in a fog. Helena stares out the window like a beautiful bird in a cage. She tells me she wants to go away for a while and that she needs a break from me. It is the hardest thing for me to say yes but that summer we go on separate holidays. She heads to Amsterdam and I reluctantly go to Fiji to avoid sitting around in our home by myself. I sit on a beach instead and do nothing for the first time in a long time.

I have to tell my wife that I'm the problem. If she stays with me she'll never be a mother. It's going to break her heart. I think about Old Jack and the way my life is in reverse. I had adolescence and became a man. Then I became a father and never got to experience it.

I'm in a beautiful paradise but it feels like I'm in hell.

I look down at the glove on my hand and for the first time in a long time consider taking it off and fading away into the sand.

I've failed.

I let tears roll down my cheeks and crash to the ground like the waves in front of me. I swim out into the ocean and float with the current.

I miss Helena.

I miss the way we both felt at the beginning when we fell in love. I miss the way things changed after we got married. The way she used to look at me made me feel complete. The waves start to pull me away from land and I realise I need to see her again.

I still love my wife.

I start to kick against the current and it takes all of my strength to get back to the beach. When I reach the shore I take a deep breath.

It's not the end yet.

I smoke weed with Doug on the morning of his wedding. The weeks leading up to this moment feel like they have unfolded in fast forward. Today feels like a good chance to talk to him about Sam and everything I've been feeling since that double date.

'Are you nervous about today?' I ask as I pack the marijuana into my old bong pipe.

'Not really man. I mean… maybe it will hit me when she is walking towards me at the altar you know? But our wedding planner Amber has been across everything so I just have to show up!'

'Does this seem *fast* to you? I mean you're still young,' I say taking a hit.

Doug looks at me with a furrowed expression.

'Seriously Ben? Are you going to try and talk me out of this on the morning of my wedding?'

I put my hands up defensively.

'No, no, no, no! It's not like that. I mean… I guess I'm just thinking about Sam and how our wedding is… like around the corner.'

'Have you guys set a date yet?' Doug asks.

'No.'

'So how is it just around the corner?'

'I guess it just feels like it's coming at me, you know? You and Jessica seem great, man. But… how do you know she's the one you want to spend the rest of your life with?'

'I just believe it.'

'And what if one day you wake up and you don't believe it anymore?' I ask.

'That's not the way it works. You can't just think about what could go wrong. You have to be open to the possibility that everything will work out for the best.'

'That's amazing man. I wish I had your confidence.'

Doug takes a hit before he speaks.

'If you're not happy with Sam then you need to talk to her.'

He smiles at me and gives me a hug.

'You've got to grow up sometime Ben. Why not today?'

'So no more weed?' I ask with a grin.

'Actually… probably not. At least not for a while. This was fun but I'd like to be able to say that the last time I smoked weed was with my best man on my wedding day.'

'Best man? But what about Patrick?'

'Patrick's not coming today. I don't know if you noticed but he was kind of a jerk. He kept flicking me in the balls too.'

'He was kind of a dick,' I say matter-of-factly.

'Ben, I don't know if I ever thanked you for saving me that night. That felt humiliating and… well... thanks.'

'It was nothing man,' I say.

'You're my best friend. I'm sorry we took a ten-year hiatus in our friendship and I'd like you to stand up there with me today.'

'I'd be honoured.'

'You don't have to make a speech or anything either. Just hold onto these rings.'

I pocket the rings and Doug throws his arms around me. We hug.

'It's going to be a beautiful day!' he exclaims.

He seems so sure that I can't debate it.

I'd never win in a million years.

Before I know it Jessica is walking barefoot down the makeshift aisle towards Doug. With each laboured step she sinks into the sand. Sam is beaming from the second row but I can't bring myself to sustain eye contact with her. Both of Doug's parents are crying. This is their finest moment. They have spent years making solid investments in property but Doug's metamorphosis from teenager to adult appears to be paying the best dividends now.

The weed has made me paranoid while Doug seems unaffected. The beach seems to move of its own accord. The crashing waves make me feel nauseous.

What hole in myself was I trying to fill all those years ago when I subjected my body to drugs and alcohol?

I know now that I was trying to find the love of my life in an effort to build the family I never had. What if I had finished my criminology degree and become more than I am now? Would I still want to be with Sam? Would we have met at all? Would I be with someone better? Would our relationship *be* better?

Doug asks me for the rings and I quickly oblige. Jessica is sobbing happily and it contagiously washes over the guests like a Mexican wave. I sneak a look at Sam and I'm surprised to find she might be the only wedding guest besides me with dry eyes. She meets my gaze and tilts her head slightly. She didn't know I would be smoking weed. Can she tell I'm under the influence? Is she judging me right now?

I wish the ground beneath me would stop swirling.

I look past Sam and into the distance. There are grey clouds forming at the other end of the beach. We should be safely inside by the time they are husband and wife.

I'll talk to Sam then.

I have to tell her that I feel like the walls are closing in on me. Maybe she feels the same way.

'I now pronounce you husband and wife. You may kiss your bride.'

Doug kisses Jessica like a hungry animal enjoying a fresh meal. I clap my hands enthusiastically even though it feels like they are kissing too much and for too long. It occurs to me that I'm losing my friend all over again. He and Jessica will drive away from this beach and start their new life together. There will be texts and occasional catch-ups but ultimately they will be their own family. I'll be stuck with Sam if things don't change.

Sam finally gets me alone on the beach after the ceremony.

'Did this give you lots of ideas for our wedding?' she asks without an ounce of subtlety.

'Actually I'd never want to get married on a beach. It seems so tacky,' I say.

'Really?' Sam asks while she folds her arms, 'I thought it was kind of romantic.'

'And… did it make you think about *our* wedding?' I ask.

'Yeah. It made me wonder why we haven't set a date yet Ben.'

'I don't know. I guess lately I've been thinking about how I'm *just* a plumber. I wish I could change everything.'

'You're more than just a plumber. And what's wrong with being a plumber anyway?'

'I mean… I just thought you would want more. I want you to be proud of me.'

'I am proud of you. I *love* you. You're going to be a great husband. And you can be anything you want to be. There's no one in your way but yourself.'

'Maybe you're right.'

'And besides… who will unclog our toilet?'

We laugh and I feel a little better.

'You're going to be a great father too.'

'I hope so.'

Sam takes both my hands and looks directly into my bloodshot eyes.

'Ben, I'm pregnant'

The heavens open and we both get drenched with rain as we scramble inside.

I'm suddenly nauseous all over again.

I feel exhausted when I finish work. The other employees take smoke breaks or coffee breaks throughout their shifts to break up the day. I neither smoke nor drink coffee but I've definitely considered taking up both just to get away from the noise. I've had a headache all day and when I'm finally finishing up I find a text message from Ally on my phone asking me 'not to call her so late at night' and four missed calls from Doug.

I call him back.

'Dude you gotta help me,' Doug says in a panicked voice.

'What's going on?'

'Not over the phone. It's really important though. Can we meet somewhere? How about when you finish work?'

Doug has an odd desperation to his voice so I agree.

We meet on a bench across from the bookshop. I'm too tired to walk across campus and I don't mind the strange stares from my co-workers. When Doug arrives I put down my copy of *Great Expectations* that I'm reading for my English class. He looks flustered as he sits down next to me.

'What's the big emergency?'

'I lost my drugs,' he says in a whispered voice.

'That sucks.'

Just go get more. You can afford it.

'I left them at the brothel,' he says leaning in with a raised eyebrow.

'What? Are you sure?'

'Do you remember the girl I told you about in the car?'

'The one in the leather?' I ask.

'Rachel, yeah. So she called me and told me she had them.'

'How did she get your number?'

'I gave her one of my business cards and told her to call me.'

Doug had a couple of hundred business cards made up last year because he thought it would help him pick up girls. He got fancy embossed black and white ones. So far I've only seen him hand them out to strippers and male students.

'So what… go and get them back.'

'It's not that simple. She wants me to buy them back from her.'

'She's blackmailing you? What a bitch.'

Ally is still on my mind.

What a bitch.

'Yeah, she said if I don't bring her five grand then she will hand the drugs and my business card to the police.'

I'm impressed. She's going to extort him and there's nothing he can do about it. Rachel sounds like an opportunist.

'So are you going to pay her? Do you have five grand that you can give away like that?'

'Yeah. I have to pay her. I can't let something like this get back to my parents. I'm going to do it tonight. I want you to come with me.'

Fuck. He can afford to just drop five grand and keep on walking.

'Why do I have to come?'

'Cos you're like a lawyer or whatever,' Doug says with a dismissive wave of his hand.

'I'm studying criminology. Not law.'

'So come and help me Ben.'

Doug is probably just asking for my help because he's scared. It's all fun and games until the police are involved.

'Also I've been drinking all morning so you have to drive the station wagon,' he adds.

No sense adding a DUI to the mix.

I agree to take him after we eat and he buys my dinner. We sit around the University cafeteria with our meals and watch students stroll past. We've opted for kebabs purely because there was no line. I'm a little worried there was no line for a reason. Maybe I should have picked law instead of criminology. I think I picked it because I have always thought about becoming a police officer. I like the idea of rules and the law. Most of the law anyway. I do think marijuana should be legalised and used for medicinal purposes. Weed has been endlessly beneficial to me in terms of my anxiety and stress.

Maybe taking Doug tonight will be a good experience. I can witness a case of extortion in person! We fill up his car with petrol and drive the required forty minutes. This trip is becoming all too familiar to me now. I decide it's not the right time to tell Doug about the blowjob I got last time.

Maybe I'll tell him on the drive back to campus.

We arrive and head upstairs to the brothel. Doug says he has been told to ask for her by name.

'Is Rachel here?' he enquires. At the desk is a woman that I haven't seen before. She's young and pale and has a sleeve featuring multiple owl tattoos.

Her eyes give him attitude but she asks him to take a seat. We have to wait twenty clock-watching minutes for Rachel to emerge, which makes me think she was definitely having sex before our meeting.

She is dressed in white cotton underwear and a see through plastic raincoat. There is a kind of white silicone tape criss-crossed over her nipples beneath the raincoat.

'Did you bring it?' she asks ignoring me completely.

'Yeah.'

If the situation were reversed I would go broke paying this woman five thousand dollars. Rachel would have asked for more if she knew his background. Doug's parents are both property moguls. They own high-rise buildings all over Australia. I've always been intimidated by their wealth. Rachel leads us down a corridor, squeaking her plastic raincoat with each step, and I scan for the faces of Michelle or Lola. I don't see them.

She takes us into a room that is dark like a dungeon with only one light hanging over the pink love heart shaped bed. I look up and spot a camera hiding in the wall pointed directly at the bed. This establishment must be well versed in blackmail. Doug can't be the first.

'Five grand?' she says impatiently.

'Yeah I've got it. But first…'

He pauses dramatically.

'…you have to fuck my friend.'

'What?' I say dumbfounded.

I'm shocked.

'Ok no problem,' Rachel says.

What the fuck?

Doug puts his arm around my shoulder and pulls me towards him.

'I didn't leave my drugs here. This was a set up. Rachel knows you're a virgin and she wants to help you with that.'

I shove him away from me.

'What the actual *fuck* Doug!'

'I've already paid for it man. I know you walked out last time and I'm sorry for tricking you into coming but you *need* this. You've got to get over this phobia you have.'

'Not like this man.'

'Then *when*? You think some perfect virgin girl is sitting at home waiting to meet you? What kind of world are you living in? Wake up. Please? Just do it. No need to thank me...'

I walk out and though Doug is calling out to me I'm no longer listening to what he's saying.

I can feel nothing but anger at being tricked. There were no drugs. Was he even drunk? I'm so tired that I can't think straight. I barrel downstairs and head for the car, pushing past faceless men as I go.

What a shitty friend.

I'm so glad that I drove. I'd rather be alone than listen to Doug's lecturing right now. As I'm about to get in the car I hear yelling and turn around.

Lola?

As much as it feels like a hallucination it's really her.

She's in trouble.

She's bleeding above her eye. Some thug in a brown jacket strikes her in the face and she falls to the dirty asphalt below. I bound over, feeling invincible and full of adrenaline from my confrontation with Doug. I've got nothing to lose and I don't care what happens next.

'Hey! Leave her alone!' I say, surprising myself with the fire in my voice.

To my surprise he stops still. The coward looks at me and puts up his hands.

'Alright, alright...' he says.

He heads into the strip club muttering something under his breath. When I'm sure he's gone I turn my attention to Lola.

I can't believe that worked.

'Are you okay?' I say trying to calm myself down.

My heart is beating faster than it ever has.

Her face is red and I feel certain she will have a black eye tomorrow.

'Thanks for the rescue,' she says trying to stand. I help her to her feet.

'What was that about?'

'Just... trouble.'

I notice her blouse is torn at the front but then I look away nervously.

'We should get you some ice.'

'No ice...I'm alright Ben.'

She knows my name.

'I'm Lola.'

'I know. I remember.'

'Do you have a car?' she says scanning the car park.

'It belongs to my friend.'

'Will you drive me home?'

'Of course.'

The song *Whose gonna drive you home?* starts to play in my head. I can't stop a smile from creeping onto my face.

Lola gets into Doug's station wagon slowly, rubbing her head, and I start the engine. Doug hasn't followed me out to the car. He's probably fucking Rachel again. He'd already paid in advance so I'm confident he wouldn't waste the opportunity. I'll take Lola home and savour the time with her.

My hands shake and I try to calm myself down.

She knows my name.

'So he's getting married in three weeks?'

Sam is predictably excited. She loves every element of a wedding and always cries during the ceremony. I've made fun of her for being such an emotional sap. We've been to four weddings in the six years we've been together. Over the course of those wedding ceremonies I have listened to countless ideas for our own eventual wedding.

'They put a bottle of rum at each table? That's tacky.'

'I love those native flowers. Remind me to have native flowers in *my* bouquet.'

'Really? That's the song they *picked* for their first dance as husband and wife?'

Our drive home is usually her chance to unpack all of her issues with the food, speeches and ceremony. Each conversation inevitably leads to us talking about our own wedding. I want it to be small and inexpensive but Sam doesn't want it to just be us signing papers at city hall. I don't want a lot of fuss and guests but Sam wants to celebrate it. She has a lot more family than I do and I feel like I'm not bringing anything to the table.

'It's not like we will ever get married again. I want everything to be perfect. I want to be together forever!'

This is what scares me the most. When I proposed it didn't feel like forever. I was in the moment. Marrying Sam feels like the natural progression in our relationship. You don't stay with someone for six years without proposing. I haven't been able to set a date though and that has been the source of all of our fighting. Most of the time we're happy but we both know it's right there and I need to shit or get off the pot.

It's not fair to Sam. It doesn't matter how I feel about it. At this stage I guess I'm getting married just to shut her up.

'Yeah three weeks. Will you be my date?' I ask taking a seat on our sofa. 'Cos I can find someone else if you don't wanna...'

'I'll be your date! What should we get them?'

'I'm not sure. It's his bachelor party next week so I'll suss it out.'

'Oooh, a bachelor party. That will be fun for you.'

Sam knows a little about my past. She knows I like strippers but she doesn't know I lost my virginity to one. She's never seen me under the influence and I never want her to. I'm completely ashamed of those years of my life.

'Sure.'

'Didn't Doug used to go to strip clubs with you?'

'Yeah, we went to a few together,' I reply carefully.

Sam doesn't know about the brothels and I don't intend on telling her.

Imagine the fight that would start!

She'd make me go and get tested – even though I have in the past and I'm totally clean. Sam would get insecure and it might ruin what we have.

I don't want her to think less of me. It's embarrassing and it's not who I am anymore.

'Do the girls get totally nude or do they keep their undies on?'

I laugh. Sam's very cute. I think she's being serious though.

'Here in Australia they get totally nude on the stage. In America they keep their undies on. I think you can go into private rooms in the back though.'

'You sound like a real expert on strippers Ben…'

I nod.

Sam starts to take off her top one button at a time.

'Do you think I would make a good stripper?' Sam asks as she moves towards me. I'm comfortable in the corner of the sofa. We have most of our sex on the sofa or in the bed so it's familiar territory.

'I like where this is going,' I say shifting myself onto the central cushion. I try and kiss Sam but she pushes me back into the corner.

'Strippers don't kiss,' she says getting into character.

'How would you know?' I ask with a grin.

She takes off her top revealing a very ordinary blue sports bra. I'm pretty sure it was purchased at Target. She takes her shorts down slowly and I'm disappointed to find that her underwear doesn't even match. Aesthetics might not seem important but it's the same as with food: you eat with your eyes first. Sam is about to climb onto the sofa when she realises the curtains are open and hurries to close them. It has a surprising effect on the mood of the room. I don't think any neighbours would have noticed since it's an odd angle to see us through the window.

'You're a shy stripper are you?' I joke as she secures the room.

'It's just that you ordered a *private* show.'

I love her for trying to stay in character. She takes her hair tie out and swishes her hair from side to side, exaggerating every movement. She's really getting into this and it's getting results. I'm becoming aroused.

Sam lifts her leg and thrusts herself near my face. I've never seen a stripper perform this move before but I'm not about to tell her that. She slides herself onto me and puts her hands on my shoulders. Sam gives a little giggle when she realises I'm turned on. She's always done that. I find it really cute, which is lucky because apparently a previous boyfriend thought she was making fun of him. I can see his point; no guy wants a girl giggling about his penis. Maybe I'm more secure about my dick than he was. It's pretty big, or so I've been told.

Sam turns herself around and lies her back down on me. She flails her arms in the air and wiggles her butt into my crotch. She slides her whole body down until she is sitting on the floor between my legs. I want Sam to take me in her mouth. She's very good at giving head if she's in the right mood. She moves up my legs now one hand at a time. I can't help but crack a smile when I see her trying to be seductive by lashing her tongue.

'What's so funny?' she asks innocently. She has no idea how hilarious she looks.

'Sorry, sorry. I can't help myself. This is too cute. Can we drop the act now?'

'I'll drop the act if you drop your pants.'

Well played Sam.

While she remains on the floor I stand and take off my pants and underwear in one movement.

'You're a lousy stripper aren't you?' she says while staring at my dick. 'Where was *my* show?'

'What can I say? I guess I got *cocky*.'

Sam laughs so hard she makes a snorting noise.

'You idiot.'

She holds my cock while she stands up like a support rail, which is strangely a turn on for me. She releases me momentarily while she takes off her underwear. Soon she's above me and I'm inside her. She feels amazing but all I can think about is how Sam is still wearing that sports bra. She moans with delight while I try and free one breast and then the other. Her nipples are forced together by the bra and I decide to lick them.

She moans louder and I want to make her come. I think I've become pretty good at sex. It helps that I've had so many sexual partners between Lola and Sam. I keep licking Sam's breasts whenever they rock towards my mouth. She stops rocking and I suck on them one at a time.

I favour the right one but I have no idea why. Each grind Sam gives becomes a subtle thrust and her breathing becomes louder.

'Oh my God.'

I'm holding out for as long as I can. The more excited Sam gets the more I enjoy it.

I feel like a stud.

She closes her eyes and her body convulses with pleasure. She releases a satisfied sigh and takes off her bra. Sam tightens herself around me. She kisses me deeply and I have no choice but to come as well.

With an invisible storm cloud over my head I start to follow people. It's a random system at first but then I actively try and seek out the worst of humanity. I head to the worst parts of town and try to find the worst people.

I want my surroundings to match my mood.

I don't feel like doing anything anymore. I spend a lot of time sitting around selecting my targets. I'll choose a populated area like a mall or a park and wait hours on my own. Other than ordering food I barely speak.

I feel like I've lost my voice.

I watch some people play the stock market and others commute to jobs they hate. I watch the daily struggle that seems to be universal. People want to have nice things and a nice home but they are forced to spend long hours suffering to reach those goals. The human race has been sold the idea of marriage and mortgage at the expense of experience. I take a large amount of money and set up an anonymous fund. Over time as I start to feel empathy for the people I follow I try to improve their lives. I send them sums of money so they might pay off their mortgages. I always pretend it is from a distant Aunt or Uncle and that they were named in their will. Sometimes I deliver the money myself. Some question the origins of the inheritance but most cheer at their good fortune.

They pay off their debts and essentially free themselves from obligation. What comes next is the part that interests me. The result of this experiment shows me that most people are changed by money.

They upgrade their lives and their social circles. Some help their families but most prove to be selfish.

I'm no different.

I was selfish too.

I'm like the unknown benefactor in *Great Expectations*. But people are greedy. I can only imagine what they would do with a time machine. The face in the mirror looks a decade older than I remember. I wish I knew how much time I had spent time travelling but I don't.

I find myself constantly regretting my decisions and trying to pulse back and fix them. I don't cross paths with myself. I don't want to see myself as a young man.

I think back to my first memories of the glove.

I wanted it to be real.

I wanted to go back and save Lola but I've been scared.

What if my first love rejects me?

What if she rejects me over and over again like Jessica did? Can I deal with the heartbreak that would certainly follow? There was a blissful ignorance that came with never seeing her again. Lola lives in my perfect memory of her.

A part of me doesn't want to sully that.

I spend nights wondering about the origins of this glove. In the future one of my great ancestors might have been working on something like a teleportation device and stumbled into time travel. Maybe once they went back they realised they could *only* go backwards and found themselves in a similar situation to my own. Everyone that ever wore the glove, no matter how many or few of them there were, now no longer exist.

They will probably never exist.

Everything will continue to move backwards.

I have changed the timeline and therefore everything is different.

I want the glove to have other functions.

I know it must.

I wish I could see a pre-recorded hologram appear like Princess Leia telling me why the glove was invented. I try countless combinations with my fingers to try and trigger some alternate function. I feel like a primitive man. I want to have a purpose but I don't. I exist here alone in the past.

It's a real mind-fuck sometimes.

Some nights I start to peel the glove off. I wonder what it would be like to die. I can never go through with it though. I think I still want to see Lola one day and the dream of being with her keeps me alive.

The glove has been a blessing and a curse. I am able to do anything I want and see any moment of my life. But I hated my life. The problem I'm having now is that I can't sleep. I see the faces from my former lives overlapping in my mind and I'm haunted with daydreams of Old Jack. He forced me back here and now I'm a man without a home.

It takes every ounce of my being to stop drinking. My binges have become dangerous and after I pulsed back and nearly landed *inside* a man on the street I knew I had to stop drinking. It's been easier this time around. I thought about calling Nathan a few times to talk but he doesn't know who I am anymore. He isn't even an AA sponsor yet.

No one is the version of themselves I want them to be.

I'm not the version of myself I want to be either.

Everything I touch still turns to shit though. I watch families gathering for dinner and think about the fact that I will never be a father. I'll never have what they have. If I ever have a child on this time travelling journey I imagine I'd meet an older version of that child shortly after. I imagine that child wearing a glove. They would see on my face that I wasn't abiding by the rules. I wasn't sending the glove back further by giving it to one of my parents. I have grown so paranoid about a child wiping me out of existence that I have stopped having sex altogether. The appetite for sex is still there but every day I try to ignore it. I'm able to put it in the background.

I don't let the monster in.

I never could have imagined giving up both sex and alcohol but that is my new reality. Sometimes I see a beautiful woman on the street or a stranger makes eye contact with me as I people-watch from a bench. It's difficult not to engage with them but I know these single serve interactions aren't real. I have become an absolute creep. I watch women undress from windows – sometimes in broad daylight.

There are no rules for me anymore.

If I'm caught I pulse away. Sometimes I *want* to be caught. I enjoy the moment a topless woman sees my face. The shock in their eyes that turns into fear and the sound of their screams still makes me feel something. Why does it take these extreme moments for me to feel anything? I guess I exist in a strange purgatory of my own creation.

I commit crimes like theft on an almost daily basis. I feel more and more detached from society. I don't care about right and wrong. I go to a football final and run naked onto the field of play. I evade the security guards to the cheers of my captive audience. I wave at them with my gloved right hand. I watch the faces of the women in the crowd as I run. They watch with open mouths as my penis flaps along with each stride. When I am about to be caught I pulse away and find myself wearing only a glove, alone in an empty stadium.

I become a nude model at an art school and delight in the giggles from the teenaged girls in the class. The male teacher seems interested too but I remain monk like in my focus. Pleasure is off the table for now. I have started to miss my boring life though. I think of Ben the plumber and wonder if his life would be better if I made sure he never dated Sam.

Would I have been just as happier in the end with someone else or is each relationship a failure in waiting?

It's a windy autumn day when Ally breezes back into my life. I find her at a University interstate that I had no idea she went to. She's more gorgeous than I remember her being. This sighting rattles me. There is an easy nature to her and she stands out in jeans and a maroon jumper. She's matured and yet she's exactly the girl I watched Buffy with all those years ago. I assume Ally changed Universities at some point after I dated her but obviously we never stayed in touch after the break up.

I never even noticed that she left.

She doesn't see me at all but passes within metres of me. I think back fondly on our time together. Why didn't we ever have sex? I can't remember anymore. Ally falls into a small category of people that I have dated and not slept with. She also predates Lola and that excites me. This lights a fire inside me again.

I want Ally to want me again.

I want to close the chapter with her by finally sleeping together. It doesn't have to mean anything. I've waited so long for a conquest that feels worthy of my time. I can pulse away like it never happened. She won't remember but I'll know. I'll have closure.

I follow Ally around campus and track her movements like a lion following a gazelle. I have flashes of an unlived life as a policeman tracking a felon. She leaves her scarf at a lunch table but I don't want to collect it.

I'm enjoying the hunt too much.

After we broke up I never really heard from her again. I checked her out on Facebook but her privacy settings were always maxed out. I wanted to say hello and be her friend again. I wanted her to miss what we were. Maybe her happiness was a façade. Maybe I could make Ally happy for a while. I was under no illusion about the journey this glove was taking me on. Everything was temporary and eventually I would travel back to the beginning. I've come around on the idea of seeing my parents. The notion of disappearing into oblivion is starting to appeal to me too.

I don't think Ally would recognise me now. I'm much older than I should be. I can't exactly introduce myself as her ex-boyfriend Ben either. She would stare blankly at me. I spend so much time imagining all the possible scenarios in my head before they happen that one afternoon, so fed up with the possibilities, I just say hello.

'Ben? Is that you?' Ally asks with a shocked smile.

'Yes. It's me.'

'You look so *different*.'

'I know. I have…a condition,' I say trying to explain the unexplainable.

She doesn't ask me to elaborate and to my surprise she's good enough to sit and talk to me.

'It's been so long! How have you been?'

'That's such a difficult question. I suppose I'm still trying to find myself.'

'Maybe you've been looking in all the wrong places,' Ally says with a smile.

I think back to the two of us kissing at University and find myself smiling back.

I take her hand in mine and she lets me. She gives a curious glance towards the glove but doesn't ask.

Ally has no more classes for the day and nowhere to be. I've started feeling a connection for the first time in a long time. I decide to take a chance.

I show her the glove.

I tell her I'm a time traveller.

It takes some convincing but eventually she believes me. Either that or she humours me.

'Okay… so you've lived *this* moment before?' she probes.

'No. This is new. I didn't know I'd see you here.'

'So what's it like? Time travel I mean.'

I should have known that she'd believe me. Ally always wanted to believe in the impossible; Vampires and immortality.

'It's…exhausting. I feel like I'm the only one rowing a boat all day and night.'

'If you don't want to do it anymore then why don't you just stop?'

I tell Ally about catching up to Jack's birth. I share my theory that another time traveller will wipe me out of existence. She ties her brown hair up into a bun as she listens intently.

'Why are you telling *me* this?' she asks when I finish talking.

'I don't know. I've never told anyone about this before. I wanted to see how it sounded out loud I guess.'

'It sounds insane, Ben. But I know you and I can see that you're telling me the truth. Or at least you *think* you are.'

'Thank you for believing me.'

'So how old are you exactly? How long have you been doing this?'

'I have no idea.'

Ally hugs me for a long time. It feels amazing to be held. It's not sexual and that's exactly what I need right now.

'Where are you staying?' Ally asks when the hug is finally over.

'Nowhere yet. I usually just check into some hotel when I feel like I need a break.'

'Come and stay with me. I'll make you dinner. I have a spare room and it would be nice to talk some more. If you're feeling up to it?'

'Alright. That sounds nice.'

When I was stalking Ally I could only think of her as a conquest. Now that I have stopped and spoken to her I remember how compatible we were as friends. Maybe she and I will go and see some live music for old times sake. She drives us back to her rental house and makes me spaghetti. I find comfort in the simple way in which her place is decorated. There are a few photos on the fridge but there is minimal furniture.

We talk over dinner about the good old days and what happened to me after Uni. Ally finds my descent into alcoholism fascinating and feels guilty for drinking her red wine in front of me.

When the night ends Ally leads me to a mattress in her spare room. She kisses me on the cheek and tells me how glad she is that I'm back in her life. When I finally fall asleep it isn't for long. I wake up to find Ally's face only ten inches from mine. I'm reminded of my night with Lola. My initial thought is that Ally wants to have sex with me. There is a certain unfinished business to our relationship that she must also be feeling.

But I'm wrong.

Ally has one hand on the glove. She has already undone the Velcro strap and now that she's seen I'm awake she desperately makes the move to pull the glove from my hand. Panic rushes through me as I clench my fist. The glove stays on my hand. I'm wide awake now.

'What are you *doing* Ally?'

Suddenly I'm shrieking in a hysterical voice I don't recognise.

'Give it to me! You had your chance. It's my turn!' she yells.

The Ally that said goodnight a few hours ago has been replaced with this insane person. She is no longer the woman I dated and watched Buffy with once upon a time. I feel myself turn red with anger as I'm filled with

a rage that I cannot control. I have been betrayed during a weak moment.
It won't happen again.

'Fuck you Ally!' I yell as I grab her by the throat.

She keeps trying to get the glove, which drives me mad. Ally has no
idea how to operate it and no idea how important it is that I keep it on. She
couldn't even use the glove if she tried. It's not calibrated for her.
I flip her underneath me and keep pressing on her neck with my thumbs.

'Stop it you idiot! Are you trying to *KILL* me?' I shout.

Why does it take these extreme moments for me to feel anything?

I let her go and stand up, still shaking from the encounter. Ally lies
completely motionless on the mattress.

She's dead.

I've never killed anyone before and I feel numb.

…

Ally's eyes stare up at me. The venom that filled them has
disappeared.

Out of some weird survival instinct I take Ally's car keys and flee
the scene of the crime. Driving through the night there is almost no traffic
on the road.

I can't believe what I've just done.

I drive to Ben Stanley's room on campus. I have started to see him
as a different person to me. I feel like we need to speak now.

I need to confront him.

I park awkwardly near the front door and brush tears from my eyes.
When did I start crying? I manage to navigate myself to the door. By the
time I start knocking my head is spinning. Ben opens the door slowly and I
stare him down. He's confused for a moment and then he's scratching his
chin as he sizes me up.

'You're a piece of shit you know?' I say, unblinking.

'What the fuck?' he manages in a groggy voice.

'Ally's dead.'

'Ally?'

'And you killed her,' I say with menace.

I'm leaning on the doorframe now.

Why can't I stay balanced?

'Huh? Who are you?'

It's a great question and I'd love to answer it but I wont. I know that I have to pulse back and avoid becoming a murderer. I could never live in this time now. I try and tell myself that she had it coming. That it was her or me. It's not true though. I might not have entered her house with murder on my mind but if anyone tries to take my glove from me I know I'll have to kill again.

'Lola's dead too you know,' I say coldly knowing that this is new information to the Ben of this time.

'How did…wait…how do you know about Lola?'

I kick my past self directly in the balls. Ben doubles over in pain. He's completely incapacitated because everything I'm carrying went into that kick.

'You're a fucking idiot Ben. You could complete your criminology degree and fight crime but you fuck around and waste your potential. You wind up becoming an apprentice plumber. Everything sucks. Everyone's going to die!'

I am shaking again. As Ben tries to sit up I start hitting him in the face. He tries to block my strikes but I'm enraged and he's already at a disadvantage.

'I hate you!' I yell as I land punch after punch.

I lean down and start to strangle Ben with murder once again on my mind. I want him to die a horrible death. I press my thumbs toward his windpipe and try to kill my past self.

I'll be fine I keep saying to myself.

I exist outside of time.

I'll survive this.

As long as I'm wearing the glove.

…

…

But I can't do it.

This isn't me.

This isn't who I want to be.

I release my grip and he gargles a mixture of blood and saliva around in his mouth. I turn around and get back into Ally's car. Ben stands up and starts trying to yell something out to me but I don't hear it. I notice a small crowd of students has gathered but no one stops me as I drive away.

Attempted Murder.

Murder.

What have I become?

Trees whiz past me as I drive recklessly into unpopulated bushland.

Almost nothing has ever made me happy. It's time to go back and save the one person who might be able to help me salvage my soul.

I'll find a quiet field and pulse back to find Lola.

I will save her and then she will save me.

Doug arrives at the pub and I give him a wave. It's a place we've both been to before and it's nice to see it has stood the test of time. I'm immune to meeting people in pubs now. Nathan and I meet in pubs all the time just to prove that we can go to them and not drink. I think it's strange that we haven't run into each other but it's possible Doug hasn't been in town. Maybe he's been scaling mountains for years. I've been quietly dreading this since the moment I agreed to meet him. Sam and Nathan thought it would be a good idea though and I tend to trust their instincts. Now that I see him up close Doug looks even better in person. He's dressed formally with a navy blue velvet jacket instead of a regular suit jacket. He throws his arms around me and pulls me into his chest.

'Benny! It's been so long!'

'Yeah man. Good to see you.'

'You look great. A little more around the old mid section…' Doug pats my stomach.

'*You* look great. I hardly recognised you. You've lost a ton of weight.'

'Yeah, I had a little heart attack and since then I've been treating my body like a temple.'

'So no more weed then?'

Weed had been such a major part of Doug's personality.

'Well… I think it made me paranoid. Although… sometimes on special occasions I have indulged.'

We order drinks and catch up. He's not drinking but assures me he *does* still drink, he's just driving today. I tell him I'm sober now.

As we both sit there with our glasses of soft drink I think about how together he seems to be. The Doug I knew just wanted to party every night. The man before me is mature. It's not long before we fall into our old rhythm and I'm feeling great about seeing him again.

'You've changed a lot Doug, but it all seems to be for the better.'

'I'm glad you think so. I look back on our University days as a pretty depressing time for me. I'll just say it, I was depressed.'

'You were?'

'I really was. I never went to see anyone about it or anything like that. I just basically lived in this cave of my own filth. I don't know whether you noticed but all I did was smoke weed, do computer coding, play video games and go to strip clubs. It wasn't much of a life.'

I think about how social I became after I stopped hanging around with Doug. I went to parties, I met people and I had sex with people. I guess I never really stopped to see how he was doing either; I just kept living my life. I remember the night I left him and took Lola home. That was a dick move. I feel really awful in retrospect.

'What happened?'

'Well I had the heart attack! It was mostly my food intake but I was also pretty stressed. A heart attack is not something you want at the age of twenty-four.'

'That's awful man. I'm sorry I wasn't there.'

'Hey, there's nothing you could have done. I was doing all the damage myself. I'm in a much better place now.'

'Well that's awesome.'

Doug sits up straight on his bar stool.

'I think I was trying to drag you down with me you know?'

'It's all good,' I say feeling the mood become serious.

'Well I just wanted to say sorry if I… you know… was a crappy friend.'

'It's in the past,' I say with a dismissive hand.

'It really is. Hey I have some news.'

'What's up?'

'I'm getting married next month and I want you to be there. If you're free.'

'Congratulations,' I say.

Doug Treborn is getting married.

I let the news sink in.

'Thanks Ben. Are you seeing someone? If you are you should bring them to the wedding.'

'Sam. She's my fiancée.'

'Congratulations right back at you! Who would have thought the two of us would be so lucky huh? I wish I could go back in time and tell that depressed stoner that everything will be fine.'

'He might not recognise you!' I say jokingly.

Holy shit. We're *adults* now. Is this what it's meant to be like? Did my father sit in a bar and catch up with his old school mates like this? At the age of thirty-two who would have thought I would be reminiscing like this.

It's weird.

'I'm sure Sam would love to come,' I say with a smile. 'She loves weddings.'

I amass another personal fortune. I find it more tedious than fun this time around. I keep my new movie mogul persona and seek out Simone McIntyre before I leave Los Angeles. Because I'm further back in the past she's a lot easier to get to this time. When I find her she is going to open auditions and bartending at night. She doesn't have a manager or an agent and though I can see the starlet she will become eventually, at the moment she looks more like the girl next door. I meet her and casually mention I'm a film producer. She asks *me* out for a drink and to my surprise she orders alcohol. I have all the power in the relationship this time and I'm surprised by how flirtatious she is. She takes me home and we have very vanilla intercourse followed by a long conversation about her hopes for a career on the stage and screen. The challenge has been taken away from me and seeing how different she used to be has put me off. Simone McIntyre is just another girl.

Maybe every girl is just another girl.

I feel tired of Los Angeles and decide to travel again. I've been thinking about my life here in my past and how meaningless it is. No one knows me and no one cares to. If I let someone in and told them about time travel they would want me to show them how I do it and then the minute I did they wouldn't remember any of it anymore. It's going to be a lonely journey into the past and I have come to terms with that.

I think about Old Jack all the time.

I wonder whether his life was like this. No wonder he was ready to wipe himself out of existence by the end. I think about the last time I saw his face and how he was aging before my eyes.

I'm haunted now by the image.

I'm running out of time too. I'm only getting older.

Soon I'll be a memory.

But who is this for? Who will remember me?

It's a double-edged sword because I have to keep time travelling back if I want to stay in existence too. If I stop and just live life in real time then eventually I assume 'parallel Ben' will meet Sam and have baby Jack just as I once did. That means Old Jack will give Ben a glove, trick him into going back and then I'll cease to be.

That's why I have to keep living in the past *before* Ben meets Sam.

I start to explore the world and seek out inspiration. I go to impoverished countries and visit slums. I'm robbed, punched and spat on in my travels and each time the trouble gets too great I use the glove. I am walking around with a get out of jail free card at all times. I meet the poorest people and see the world through their eyes.

Is this how the world works?

I feel myself wishing there was a better life for them all but knowing that even if I help them now it would mean nothing the next time I pulsed away. Nothing is permanent if I use the glove. Maybe when the glove gets far enough into the past someone will change something so big that the whole world will change. It's humbling to think about being a part of such an event. It's maddening to not know what this glove is for.

I feel tired all the time. The obligation to do something with myself creates an unusual pressure. I complete several lifetimes' worth of bucket lists but there is nobody to share it with. I try to focus on temporary friendships.   I find assorted companions in Argentina, Canada and New Zealand with inevitable results. If I stay with them I can't tell them about the glove, if I stay too long I worry that I'll be erased by my parallel self. It's now impossible to know how old I am because I keep folding time over onto itself. I no longer celebrate birthdays and there are no markers on the way. I estimate that I'm approaching thirty-seven but I might be closer to forty. Sometimes I feel ninety.

Once during a drunken storm in Belgium I took the glove almost completely off. My hand was wrinkled and dry underneath. It was so pale and unrecognisable. Within a matter of seconds my heart started beating faster in my chest. I could feel my extremities stretching and contracting all at once. My eyes started to hurt and I put the glove back on.

I hate Old Jack and regularly curse his name. He haunts only me. Old Jack has never existed to anyone but me and now I vow that he'll never exist again as I travel back towards my own birth. I'll give the glove to a parent, say goodbye to the world and before I know it I'll be just like him.

A memory.

Possessions become meaningless to me. Everything in this world is only borrowed. Each time I travel I lose it all again so I learn to do without. After the first time I pulsed back I realised I had some coins in my wallet. They were minted with the year Jack was born. I carry them with me through every pulse I make as they mark the moment my life changed and serve as my own private proof of my story. I don't know if I'll ever need them but they are tokens that remind me this story is bigger than me.

I become vegan for a time and feel better but miss meat and go back. I shave my head, grow a beard and evolve my appearance. I spend time with religious figures and learn the differing religious beliefs of the world. I walk the Earth and try to help people even though it's only temporary. It makes me feel that much better about my journey. I hear the same songs go up and down the charts and experience the déjà vu of their popularity. I hear about the same celebrities dying and the same scientific discoveries. I'm not surprised by anything anymore.

I am Brad Dumas the time traveller.

A man without a home, without a family and without limits. I wish I had enjoyed my life more before the glove tightened around my hand. I wish I had tried to make it work with Sam. I wish I had made different choices. I really wish it hadn't taken me years in isolation to realise that I was living my life all wrong.

I'm in India when it really hits me. My life had meaning when I was younger. I had friends like Doug and the seedlings of a life. Those relationships were earned.

I need to go back and see myself.

I will enjoy my life from afar as an observer. I'll be my own guardian angel and make sure I'm okay. I'm so tired of having no direction whatsoever that any plan feels like progress.

When I travel back I land during my most shameful and drunken days. I'm too old to be drinking at a University bar but I find myself there anyway.   I watch Ben Stanley buy himself drink after drink. He's trying to make tonight the best night ever. Chasing an uncatchable high.

I observe my terrible drunken behaviour.

I see moments I was never privy to before now.

I see the looks and I pity myself.

It's not easy to endure so I leave.

I find Doug smoking weed outside. I don't let him see me. I sense he would be the only one here that could identify me. I follow him home and find myself obsessively stalking my friend. I watch Doug for about a month without detection. I see memories that I have blocked out. Doug confronting Ben about his drinking and then getting punched in the face for his trouble. It turns out I wasn't a good friend to Doug at all.

I was a fucking jerk.

No wonder he stopped talking to me.

Finally one day while following my friend I see him sit down at a café and start talking to an elegant woman. It's his future wife Jessica and this is the moment they meet for the first time. *Or is it?*

'You have to buy the bouncer a drink,' Lola says with the closest thing to a smile I have seen from her so far. I love her accent.

'Okay, what should I get him?'

'Double rum and coke. That's his drink.'

I head to the bar and scan the room. It's fairly full considering the time. The gold curtains look as cheap as some of the talent. There is a team of men surrounding a gyrating dancer. She is favouring a man with a red leather jacket to the side of the stage. It's odd because the men are watching him as much as they are watching her. She flashes her crotch at the man and they scan his face for a reaction. Sometimes it's what you don't see that is the sexiest. This psychological experiment only lasts a few minutes before the men start to get rowdy again. She acknowledges their need for flesh and presses her breasts into his face and they all look on in envy. He is the chosen one. Maybe he just has the most money to spend.

I decide I'll get Lola something from the bar too. The drinks are probably overpriced but when I mention the double rum and coke is for the bouncer the chump behind the bar gives me a funny look. He thinks I'm a friend of the establishment and gives me all three drinks for free. I deliver the first drink to the bouncer and return to Lola with two beers.

'I don't really drink,' she says as she waves her hand at the beer casually.

'Oh right. Because you're working?'

'I'm six months sober,' she replies. 'And I'm not working anymore tonight.'

People must try to buy her drinks all the time. No big deal. Two drinks for me then. I could use the courage.

'So what do you do?' she asks looking past me at the dancing girls.

'I'm studying criminology,' I reply, hoping she'll be impressed.

She isn't.

She nods a few times and then looks around the room without a word.

Lola takes her packet of cigarettes and passes them to the bartender casually.

'So what's it like working upstairs?' I say trying to continue the conversation.

What's it like being a *prostitute*? What am I asking her?

'I don't fuck people for money.'

She's offended. I've fucked this up in record time.

'Sorry, I just thought… I mean I *saw* you up there.'

'And you thought I was a hooker?' she says unwrapping some gum.

'I guess I did. I've never been upstairs before so I don't really know what a hooker is supposed to look like.'

She stares at me for a beat and chews her gum.

Yes, I'm really just this naïve. Please believe me because that's the truth.

'I was just hanging out,' Lola says defensively. 'My friend works up there.'

'Oh.'

I wonder if her friend is having sex with my friend. That would be weird. I swallow the urge to make this observation. I'm so glad I didn't try to pick her. That would have been so embarrassing.

A funny story to tell the grandkids about?

'So are you a bartender?' I ask trying to keep her talking.

'I'm a stripper.'

'Cool,' I say, trying to be the most laid back version of myself. I can feel my face getting red as I drink one beer and hold the other. I must look ridiculous with a beer in each hand.

'How's the beer?' she asks, eyeballing me.

I can't tell if she's just being polite or if she misses the taste of beer so much that she needs to know how it tastes to me. I play it down.

'Good thanks. So do you *like* stripping?'

'I'm told I'm quite good at it,' Lola says matter-of-factly.

'There is a certain art to taking off clothes,' I say. 'Not everyone can do it. I try to get dressed and undressed at *least* once a day.'

I'm being playful which means the beer is working.

'What I mean is… not everyone will *pay* someone to strip.' Lola says passionately.

'That's true. I've been in here for ten minutes and I haven't paid anyone to strip! I might make an exception for you though… now that I know you're quite good at it.'

'Well you know where to find me.'

I've finished my first beer and my buzz is back. The patrons seem to have thinned out but that might be because they are in the back rooms. There are lots of dark corners for private shows. The large dim room behind the stage is divided into sections. Each section has leather seats where men are being given lap dances. There are several beefy security guards watching to make sure no one breaks the rules.

'Are you just stripping to put yourself through school or something?' I ask.

It's a cliché.

The stripper with the heart of gold.

Julia Roberts in *Pretty Woman*. Well, she was actually a prostitute in that film but she did have the heart of gold. I guess I'm just hoping to find some common ground with Lola.

'Nope. Gotta pay the bills somehow, and this is working out pretty well so far.'

'Plus you're good at it,' I add with a thumbs up.

'That's what I'm told! Are you going to get a lap dance? There are lots of good girls working tonight.'

'I don't know. Would you recommend anyone?'

Lola looks around.

'Do you see those two girls near the bar?' she asks pointing.

The first girl is short but has a muscular little body. A real pocket rocket. Her dark hair is in pigtails and she has a kind of a Britney Spears schoolgirl look to her. I recognise the second girl from her performance earlier. Her previously exposed breasts are now housed in a black bra with a pink bow on it. She has matching underwear and stockings. Her clothing seems ill fitting but I guess it won't be staying on for very long.

'Yeah I see them.'

'They are working the room right now, going from one guy to another seeing if anyone wants a lap dance.'

'How much would a lap dance set me back?'

'Thirty dollars for two songs.'

Thirty dollars for about six minutes work. Three hundred dollars an hour. I wonder what the girls upstairs are making.

The girls spot Lola and give her a polite wave. She nods to them and chews her gum with her mouth open. She makes a big gesture and points to me.

'This is Ben and he wants a lap dance,' Lola says loudly.

Their eyes light up with delight. The schoolgirl does a series of quick claps as she bounds over. I'm too nervous to argue.

'Hi Ben, I'm Nikki,' says the pocket rocket. 'This is Willow.'

Willow looks me up and down quickly while she pulls her loose bra strap back onto her shoulder.

'Nice to meet you,' I say after I finish off my second beer.

'So would you like a lap dance?' Willow asks.

'Sure.'

I'd like a lap dance from Lola but I guess this will do. If I say no I'll seem like some kind of voyeur. Or that I'm a tight arse. I have to roll with this. I don't want to get on her bad side.

'Who did you want?' Lola asks me.

You.

I think about saying both of them but as a student I can't afford it. Nikki looks a bit too child-like for me. Plus she is covering a lot of skin so I have no idea what she looks like under there. I'm better off sticking to what I know. Willow is busty and I'm a breast man.

'Willow was it?'

Lola smiles genuinely for the first time. I seem to have earned some kind of hidden respect points for validating her profession or supporting her friends. Willow links arms with me and leads me past the stage to the dark of the back room. The security guard smiles at Willow without even looking at me.

'Nice talking to you cutie,' Lola calls out.

She thinks I'm cute. Tonight has not been in vain.

I collapse into an oversized chair and brace myself for what is about to happen.

'Do you have some money for me?' Willow says cheerfully.

I hand over the thirty dollars. I wonder how much of that goes to her. I look around but none of the chairs are facing mine. If there were any other patrons back here the room would be too dark for me to see them. The room has a lemony smell that stirs up images of rubber gloves and cleaning products. Willow scrambles on top of me leaving no space between us. I can feel myself getting hard almost immediately. She must feel it too and gives me a polite smile. Something about her poise makes me feel like I'm in good hands and Willow seems like the kind of girl that likes to be in control. Maybe she appreciates the power that strippers wield over men like me.

'I'll just wait til this song ends,' she whispers in my ear while remaining in my lap.

I love this. The anticipation is amazing.

'Just so you know I work for tips,' she adds reminding me that this is a transaction.

How professional.

'Sure,' I say quietly. I think I needed that reminder.

Without asking she runs her hand up and down the front of my jeans stroking the length of my cock.

'You're not going to *stiff* me are you?'

Holy shit.

'No,' I manage to say despite my complete shock.

A new song finally starts and like a coin operated ride so does Willow. I'm hard as a rock. She removes her top layer and presses her breasts into my face. It's tempting to open my mouth as her nipple glides past my lips but I resist my basic urges. She places her bra around my neck and slowly grinds against me.

'I can't… *touch* you… can I?' I ask timidly.

It doesn't hurt to ask. Maybe it's allowed and I'm missing my chance.

'No. Sorry hon. Unless you want your fingers broken.'

The bouncer is lurking somewhere out there in the darkness.

'You can touch me though. That seems unfair,' I offer pointing out the inequality.

'You liked that didn't you?' she asks with a smile.

She's loving everything about this. In truth I'm loving it too. I grip the chair, wishing I could grab her butt. She lets the bra drop to the floor and slides her hands down my torso suggestively. She stands and turns herself around. Willow backs up and parks herself in my lap. She slides her hand down the inner seam of my jeans and brushes it dangerously close to my balls. Her underpants have slid down just a fraction and her butt is more tempting than ever. I imagine her routine is a perfect simulation of what sex must be like. It is certainly amazing foreplay if nothing else. She has started grinding slowly now and it feels so good. She leans forward and touches the floor at the base of the chair. I feel like I'm having her doggy style. When she comes back up again she looks back at me and clutches her breasts. She smiles.

'Does that feel good?'

I nod, unable to speak.

She leans down towards the floor again only this time she squeezes my cock gently with her hand. Her body hides everything she does. I let out a moan that only Willow is close enough to hear.

'Does *that* feel good?'

I come.

I don't even last one full song.

I can feel the liquid sliding down my groin. It feels like a lot and I'm suddenly really self-conscious that it will stain through my underwear and onto my jeans. I can't go back to Lola with a wet patch on my crotch. I look up and into the eyes of Willow. She has repositioned herself to face me. She knows exactly what's just happened. When my life flashes before my eyes at the moment of my death I feel like this moment might make an appearance.

'Hi,' she says with a satisfied grin.

The cat that got the cream.

Now that she has gotten me off I want her to get off of me.

'That was nice,' I say hoping she will give me some space.

'A tip would be nice too. I don't do that for every customer.'

I give her a bunch of notes from my wallet and slowly move for the bathroom.

Inside it's absolutely gross from top to bottom. The tiles that were once a shade of white now resemble the bowels of the men that have frequented this cubicle. It's possible that someone has recently crapped in their hand and then written their name on the wall to my left. It looks like his name is 'Ronnie' but the text is hard to read. I take off my underwear and survey the damage. This is beyond embarrassing. I try to clean up as best I can but this might be the end of the road for them. I don't think I can wear these again in their current condition. It is at this moment that my phone starts vibrating.

Doug must have finished with the girl in the leather.

I put my jeans back on and leave the cubicle. I throw my underwear into the rubbish bin and look at myself in the graffiti stained mirror. There is thankfully no evidence on the front of my jeans.

As I head outside to the car to meet my friend I look for Lola but she's nowhere to be seen. Probably outside having another smoke. Maybe I'll see her out there and say goodbye. I can thank her for the recommendation. When I get past the bouncer and into the cold night I spot Doug sitting in his car. He waves me over.

There's no sign of Lola.

'Where were you man?' he asks as I get into his station wagon.

'I was in the strip club. Downstairs.'

'Did you get done *early*?' he smiles flicking his greasy hair behind his ears.

He's implying I didn't last long. He doesn't know how quickly I ran out of the brothel. Technically I did just come in my pants within a three-minute song, so he's not too far from the truth.

'I couldn't go through with it Doug.'

'Awww… next time bud. Weed?'

He holds out a joint and I shake my head. Doug is a bit of a stoner but it doesn't seem to affect his driving. It doesn't bother me anymore. My mind is elsewhere. I am wondering if Willow is inside somewhere telling Lola about our lap dance. The forty-minute drive feels like hours as Doug tells me minute by minute about his latest sexual experience.

I think about Willow.

I think about Lola.

I think I need a real girlfriend.

One that exists in the daylight hours.

It's the night of the bachelor party and I'm dressed in a black shirt and brown pants. I'm going because I feel good about reconnecting with Doug last week and I haven't met his best man Patrick or his future brother in law Michael. This could be really awkward if they ask why I'm not drinking or try and force alcohol onto me.

I won't drink.

I won't be peer pressured into it. The days of waking up with fractured memories, strange voicemails and unexplained bruises are gone. I hear a car horn and head out the front of my place. Doug is in a taxi waving at me.

'How are ya Ben?' he asks happily. I don't know why he is in such a good mood but I hope it's infectious. I could use a fun night out and a break from my weekly grind.

'Pretty good man. Are you ready for your last night as a free man?'

'Yeah right. My fiancée is going to hear about everything that happens tonight. I promised I wouldn't do anything *too* crazy.'

'Cool. I'll be taking it easy too. Should be fun,' I say optimistically. I want Doug to have fun.

Going to a strip club is something I haven't done in years. Why would I need to? As far as I'm concerned being around nearly naked women helped turn me into some kind of sex-addicted idiot once upon a time. The alcohol gave me no filter and I remember burning through my savings in about six months. I would try and pick up every woman I met and my success rate was unfortunately high which meant my behaviour went on longer than it should have.

'Patrick and Michael are both at the strip club already so we'll meet them there.'

'No worries.'

'To be honest they are both going to be drinking heavily tonight so I'm guessing they will have a pretty big head start.'

'Sure.'

Doug gives me a quick tap with the top of his hand.

'How is work anyway?'

'Work is boring man. You don't wanna hear about it.'

'Alrighty. No shoptalk. Let's just make memories.'

Whenever I think about strippers it's impossible not to think about Lola. I often think about the night I had sex with her. She's burned into my brain. I wonder where she is and who she's with tonight. I think about her breasts and her legs and all the times she let me make love to her that night when I was on Viagra. I miss her and I didn't really know her. I often think about how that brief encounter shaped my University days. If I hadn't met her and had sex maybe I would be a police officer right now. Maybe I would have been a hero and saved the Prime Minister. Maybe I would have been shot in the line of duty and died a virgin.

We arrive at the strip club and step out of the taxi. The neon lights are blinding and it's starting to rain. Doug pays a cover charge for us both, which he insists on, and we head inside. It's a pretty standard looking strip club. The music is blaring. The majority of the patrons are male except for the two or three women who are 'trying something different' or 'spicing things up.' The floors are sticky and I try to imagine a drink was spilled here instead of something more unsavoury.

My eyes wander to the stage and I'm pleasantly surprised to see a woman spinning around upside down. She is a blur of motion surrounded by men. They sit silently hoping for something but not knowing what they actually want. She stops at the bottom of the pole and crawls toward a man in a grey t-shirt. He gulps as she presses her breasts into his eye line. He withdraws his wallet and tucks a pile of notes into the woman's G-string happily. She gyrates on the stage like a wind up toy and no one can look away.

This all gets interrupted when a man comes up and lightly punches Doug in the balls. I quickly learn this man is Patrick and this must be how he normally says hello.

'G'day,' I say quickly and shake his hand. 'Ben.'

'I'm Patrick.'

He's definitely been drinking and looks like he's having a great time. He has sandy blonde hair and a huge grin. I can't tell if he has an extra large mouth or extra teeth.

'Patrick and I work together,' Doug shouts to me over the music.

He goes on to tell me something about developing an app together but I'm not really listening. Several strippers have walked past me now and each one has either smiled or touched my arm.

'Where's Michael?' Doug asks Patrick loudly.

'Taking a piss.'

Patrick ushers us over to the corner with the only couch. It's a two-man couch so I sit up on the armrest awkwardly instead of trying to squeeze in.

'Alright! Bachelor party baby!' Patrick says enthusiastically.

'Take it easy. We've got all night,' replies Doug as he scans the room.

A man leaving the bathroom heads straight for our group. This must be Michael. He looks awkwardly out of place as he heads in our direction.

His beard is exceptionally long, as if he lost a bet, and his hands are full of beer. I mentally compare Nathan's beard with Michaels and rank

Nathan's more impressive because it feels like an intentional choice rather than a prop. Michael returns to us via the bar and when he arrives sets four beers down on the small table in front of our couch.

'Hey mate, you must be Michael,' I say, trying to sound friendly.

'Nice to meet you. Ben, right?'

'Yeah.'

We shake hands and I'm impressed with his grip.

'I got you all beers,' he says. Normally beer is just the right social lubricant for this situation but unfortunately I have to refuse.

'No thanks, I don't drink.'

'You don't *drink*?' he repeats with a puzzled look. I shake my head. Patrick picks up two beers and shoves them into Doug's open hands.

'Catch up Dougie boy!'

Doug silently starts to chug the beers as I turn my attention back to Michael who is inexplicably still standing.

There is a seat right next to Doug.

'So what do you do with yourself Michael?'

'I'm a swimming teacher,' he replies with some disdain.

I nod. I imagine his beard floating on the top of the water while he bobs up and down. I have no follow up questions for him. Luckily a couple of girls come up to our little group before it gets awkward.

'How are you boys doing tonight?' shouts the one dressed as a horny devil.

'Anybody interested in a lap dance?' asks the one dressed as a slutty angel.

They sit down on the small table across from the sofa without regard for the cleanliness of the surface. Patrick starts asking questions while

Doug squirms in his seat. Michael has been standing the whole time and looks like he isn't even with us. He strokes his beard as he watches the girls on the stage in the distance. Doug finishes his beers and burps into his hand. Patrick seems like he has big plans for Doug's bachelor party and he's trying to enlist our new friends. I can't hear what he's asking the girls but he keeps pointing back at Doug. Eventually Doug waves the girls away and Michael and I lean in to hear him speak.

'Guys I know it's *my* bachelor party but I want us *all* to have a great time.'

'I'm having a great time buddy!' Patrick says as he ruffles Doug's hair.

'I don't need to be the centre of attention… really… so I thought I would buy you guys a dance,' he says taking out his wallet. What a concept! The would-be groom buying lap dances for everyone else at *his* bachelor party. I understand Doug's dilemma. This is set to be an embarrassing night for him and he's trying to bribe us. He can bankroll this evening if he wants - I wont stop him. After he's given each of us a fistful of cash he offers to get the next round and no one protests.

When he walks away Patrick sidles over to me.

'Can you believe it?'

'What?'

'What a fuckup! If we pool our money we can pay a stripper to do some *really* fucked up shit to him!' Patrick snatches the money from Michael and I and bounces out of his seat happily. Michael finally sits down and we strike up a conversation.

'So Michael, Doug's marrying your sister?'

'Yeah. Jessica.'

'He's a good guy. I'm sure he'll make a good brother in law. Like if you need an app developed.'

'Or if we need a loan?' Patrick says holding a fist full of money.

I chuckle half-heartedly. Suddenly I realise I have listed all the things I know about Doug. Since we drifted apart I don't know anything about his day-to-day life. He's getting married to Jessica, he creates apps and he's well off. Michael asks about my job and specifically if I can come over one day and replace a washer for him. I tell him yes even though I assume this scenario will never eventuate. When Doug returns with two soft drinks and a beer I watch as Patrick gets up to 'take a lap.'

I take the opportunity to tell him about Patrick's plan to pool the money.

'Really?' he says with disappointment splashed across his face.

'Yeah, he's pretty into the idea,' I say.

'Of getting a girl to do something fucked up to me?'

'Yeah,' I say.

Doug takes a sip of his coke and shakes his head. It's not the worst thing that might happen tonight. He could wake up in a dress handcuffed to a pole outside a police station. He could wake up on a plane without his wallet. I'm going to avoid getting a lap dance. No drinking and no lap dances. I'm bucking all the trends. I've come so far in terms of my sobriety and I can't chance a relapse. I'm trying to keep my beautiful fiancée Sam in mind as I turn down each casual offer from a stripper.

Patrick returns with a woman of about thirty. She introduces herself as Jessica, which freaks out Doug immediately.

'Ha! I told her to say that!' laughs Patrick maniacally.

She gives everyone a shrug and smiles until Patrick is finished cackling.

'I'm Wendy,' she says sitting down on Doug's lap. She's wearing a little top that reveals her midriff and a short skirt.

I can see it is attached with press-studs for quick removal. Her hair is black with bleached blonde streaks. She touches Doug's face and strokes his hair as she speaks.

'Your friend has asked me to do a dance for you. Come into the back room.'

Doug is reluctant but he stands up, holding Wendy's hand as they walk away.

'Come on,' calls Patrick. 'We're ALL going to watch!'

Reluctantly Doug stands and shuffles himself through a colourful curtain of beads. We find two smaller areas divided with darker curtains. One has a security guard blocking the entrance so we instinctively head for the other. Inside Doug is parked in an oversized chair while Wendy dances in front of him. Her skirt is discarded to reveal a lacy black G-string. She starts including us in the show as she moves around the private room. We all sit down on a surprisingly uncomfortable wooden bench that is too close to the wall. Doug looks suitably nervous but he's having an okay time. Wendy removes her top theatrically and waves it above her head. Her body is tanned and seemingly flawless. She takes off her bra to reveal two very fake breasts. Perhaps it was flawed after all.

Wendy moves to the wall behind us and takes a plastic covered crash mat back to Doug. She commands him to lie down on it. There must have been a version of this without the crash mat once. I imagine the floor in the back room of a strip club probably isn't the most hygienic. I think about how many times that crash mat might have been wiped clean.

When did I become such a germophobe?

Wendy collects something from a nearby woven basket. She covers it with a black handkerchief and brings it back. Doug lies down and Wendy straddles him. She pulls his jumper up over his head and tells him to leave it there so he can't see what she is doing. She starts rocking on him while looking at Patrick and I. Wendy is trying so hard to include us in the experience. She bites one of Doug's nipples until he cries in agony.

When she lets go there are deep teeth marks on him. Wendy looks back at us for validation. I have the sensation that she's been possessed by something evil. I don't know how to react.

'You like that?' she says before she repeats the process on the other nipple.

Doug tries to pull down the jumper but Wendy shouts at him not to. His chest has started turning red. She turns herself around to face Doug's feet and starts undoing his belt. I look over and see Michael stroking his beard and looking at his phone. He's either not into this at all or he's snapping photos covertly. Wide-eyed Patrick, on the other hand, loves every moment. Wendy senses the energy of the room and starts playing to Patrick. She undoes Doug's belt and fly. Doug sits up in protest for a moment, jumper still covering his face, before lying back down. Patrick jumps off the wooden bench and grabs Doug's cock in his hand.

'You turned on yet Doug?'

'What the fuck!' Doug replies suddenly. 'Is that you Patrick? Don't touch my dick.'

'That's a YES! He's got a boner for you Wendy!'

'I don't,' Doug protests feebly.

I don't *think* he is aroused. I think Patrick must *think* Doug is turned on because of his own tiny cock. Maybe this whole thing is over-compensating from Patrick. I'm suddenly glad I'm not the one lying there with my fly undone. I definitely would have been turned on and it would have been obvious to everyone. This kind of shit makes me nervous for my own wedding. I would rather go see a music festival or do paintball but for some reason a bachelor party isn't complete without humiliation and strippers. If I ever wind up marrying Sam maybe I'll tell her I don't want a bachelor party at all.

Wendy runs her fingernails down Doug's thighs and then grazes the inside of his pants. Doug might be getting turned on now and Patrick can't stop staring at him. Could he be gay? I don't have a good radar for this and honestly have no idea. Wendy seems pleased with herself and reaches for the basket. She reveals its contents: *hot wax*. Michael is paying attention again.

'This just got interesting,' he says quietly so only Patrick and I can hear.

Wendy stands up and drips the hot wax onto Doug's exposed torso. He screams in pain and she starts to laugh. Patrick laughs too.

I stand up and instinctively grab Wendy, pulling her away from Doug.

'Fucking hell,' Doug cries as he rolls his body around in pain.

'Hey! No touching!' Wendy yells at me.

I'm pissed off.

Without thinking I knock the wax to the floor and carry her out of the room over my shoulder. She's gone too far and Doug is hurt. To my surprise there is no security guard outside our room when we get through the curtain. I put Wendy down and she slaps me in the face.

'What the fuck *arsehole*?'

'You poured hot wax on my friend!' I retort, trying not to spit as I speak.

'Your other buddy *paid* me to do that! He *asked* me to! I figured you all knew what I was doing. Isn't he into that kind of kinky stuff?'

'No.'

I wasn't sure though. I really don't know Doug at all. Maybe he's into that. He definitely didn't seem to enjoy it though.

'You don't touch me again. You of all people know not to touch strippers.'

You of all people.

'What do you mean?' I ask.

'Fuck you.'

'What do you mean *I* should know better?'

'You don't remember me do you?' Wendy asks with fire in her eyes.

'No,' I reply.

'We all know you from a few years ago. You used to come in here all the time. You were always drunk but you were a big tipper so we put up with you. You got roughed up by the bouncers a few times when you touched the girls… inappropriately.'

I feel a flush of shame. My blackout drunk years are coming back to haunt me.

'That's not all,' she continues, 'the girls talk about you like some kind of urban legend.'

Oh God.

'Once while you were getting a lap dance you were so drunk you pissed yourself.'

It's brutal to hear. She's telling me about a time in my life I can't recall.   I sound like a disrespectful monster. I listen patiently as she destroys any dignity I thought I had. She gets so close to me that I can feel her breath when she exhales in anger. It's not sexual. I feel like I have to let her finish. She berates me and calls me names. I see Patrick poke his head out to see what's going on. He decides not to interrupt and disappears shortly after. Finally when a security guard does come over to check on us Wendy waves him away. She can handle me all by herself.

'Why don't you fuck off and *die*?' she concludes before storming off.

Sometimes I think I need this. It feels terrible when it's happening but it is more therapeutic than AA. I'll bottle this moment and break it down next time I chat to Nathan. I'm always being reminded why I needed to stop and why it's important that I don't drink again. I return to the boys alone. Patrick is shitty that I stopped the show but Doug gives me a short pat on the shoulder and thanks me.

'You're welcome.'

I'll go home and tell Sam that I had fun. I'll tell her Patrick is kind of a douchebag and that Michael is shy. I'll tell Sam that I'm looking forward to the wedding. If she asks I'll tell her I'm too tired to fuck.

Maybe tomorrow I'll wake up and feel less like a monster.

I pulse back and watch myself again. Filling in the holes in my past has become my new addiction. I'm in awe of my past confidence with women. I have to wait a while before Ben and Nellie's night comes around again. I can't believe I was with such a beautiful woman that I really don't remember at all. I want to see how it ended. I wait patiently behind a tree as each taxi comes to a stop at the red light.

The night air is crisp but I don't mind waiting. I'm a very patient time traveller these days.

Eventually I spot them spilling out of the taxi and my heart accelerates. The driver yells out at them but doesn't give chase. I watch as they come closer and closer to my hiding spot. We are in a suburban street and I'm guessing this must be where Nellie lives. Nothing seems familiar to me. They keep looking behind them but there is no one following them but me.

Nellie makes several playful gropes at Ben's jeans and definitely squeezes his cock more than once. How in the hell did I suppress this? Maybe the drinking finally got so bad that my brain cells died.

Maybe the time travel has given me amnesia.

Alternatively maybe in my prime this was a normal Friday night. I'd had sex with lots of women after Lola. I remember that after each conquest I would think of her. I wondered if Lola had moved away and whether she'd come back. I wondered if our paths would randomly cross again. I missed her.

Ben and Nellie make their way down a short driveway and while she fumbles for keys he grabs her by the waist.

A stick breaks beneath my feet and I freeze. They haven't heard me. They head into the house and turn on a light.

They are out of my sight now.

I check the street for witnesses but it is late and everyone else must be asleep in bed. This evening has a dreamlike quality to it. I creep up to the window but can't see them. They must be at the back of the house. I make my way as silently as possible over the side gate and hear the bark of a dog in the distance. The backyard is plain and I am thankful Nellie doesn't have too many obstacles for me to contend with. When I reach the bedroom window I see a lamp with red material covering it. It reminds me of the red light district in Amsterdam. Ben is sitting on the bed facing away from the window but Nellie is nowhere to be seen. While I wait I study my younger self.

Ben looks like he is bored.

He doesn't appreciate what he has in front of him.

His eyes dart from wall to wall studying the various posters and photos that Nellie has chosen to display.

The bathroom door opens and Nellie walks back into the room. She is topless now and her curvy figure is bathed in the red glow of the lamp. She is still wearing jeans but has them unbuttoned at the front exposing the front of some black underwear. She moves like a jungle cat towards the bed before turning back around and walking away again. She's like a runway model. Ben tries to grab her as she approaches but each time she makes him sit back down. Nellie stops near the bed and turns sideways. She pulls the jeans down to the floor in a practiced way and steps out of them. Nellie sways from side to side in her tiny black panties.

Watching this confident woman is breathtaking. She runs her hands over her breasts as I undo my pants. She bites her fingers as I start stroking my cock. She straddles Ben and presses him down on the bed. She takes off his pants and starts to touch him. Everything she does to him I try to repeat on myself. When she puts Ben's dick between her breasts it is all too much and I come against the brick wall of the house. I realise I have been breathing heavily on the window and quietly wipe it clean.

What am I doing?

I watch my past self fuck Nellie in missionary position and then leave. I watch her lie in bed alone, thumb through a magazine and then fall asleep. I feel strange about how quickly Ben discarded her and ashamed at how I must have forgotten her. This woman is representative of all of the women I've wronged. I've never seen the aftermath of a night with me.

This is a sobering moment.

Now that I know where Nellie lives I find myself drawn to learn more about her and her world. I pulse back and watch her alone in her room.   I feel disgusted at how much I enjoy this voyeurism. Why can't I stop watching her? I feel so guilty. She makes a lot of phone calls. Nellie seems to be lonely. I watch her bring men home and have sex with them. I watch until it makes me sad. I didn't want to meet her. I feel like I only used her for sex. The guilt of not even remembering that night makes my stomach churn. After I have observed enough of Nellie I go back to watching myself.

I was going off the rails. I was getting too old to be drinking and partying all the time but I was still oblivious to my problem.

I watch myself drink and skip University classes.

I was failing at everything and I was too close to see it.

I watch Doug tell me that I need to stop being stupid.

'Don't be so reckless.'

I remember thinking he was trying to ruin my good time but really he was a good friend and I couldn't acknowledge his help. When I get to the beginning and find my parents it will be sad that none of this will exist but it will be for the best. I made so many juvenile mistakes that scarred me. At least a complete reset will mean that my mistakes will be undone.

I spend a long time looking at the glove. I attempt touching different fingers together with no obvious results. If it has other functions I cannot seem to trigger any of them. I remember Old Jack saying some features were disabled. Could I find a way of enabling them? Going backwards through time is useless if you can't go forwards too. I have been struggling to see the logic in this invention at all. Did my ancestors intend for me to stop 9/11 or for my grandparents to kill Hitler? Was there a purpose to this glove being created and have we lost it? I remember Old Ben saying the phrase *Chinese Whispers across generations* and it all feels impossibly hard. I can't figure out a way to go forward so I'll never know why.

Time travel has made me emotional. I think it is due to a lack of sleep and regulated activities. I can't measure time and therefore have no sense of it. I look in the mirror and the face I see looks haggard. I'm carrying the stress of the world through time with me.

I'm watching myself one night at a bar near the University when I see two drunken girls dancing near me. I remember immediately that this was the night of our threesome. They look as fantastic now as they do in my memory. I watch them chat to friends and talk about heading home. I see the scene from a new angle and find them scheming towards a threesome well before I was in the loop about it.

I overhear their names.

Becca and Chloe.

Details of the night start to come back to me.

I remember Becca was the third wheel. After I'd managed to get them both back to my place I remember she sat watching Chloe and I hook up on the sofa. She was awkward but I found the whole thing really hot. I was content to sleep with Chloe while her friend watched.

Chloe kept ignoring Becca. She was really in the moment. When Chloe took off my pants to reveal my cock I remember hearing an audible gasp from Becca.

I'll always remember that gasp.

She was quiet after that.

Chloe started blowing me and I kept looking at Becca. It made her work me harder and harder, seeking my approval, trying to make me come while urging me to look at her. It felt amazing. I lay back and thrust my groin forward. To my surprise Becca joined in and suddenly I had two mouths, four hands and the biggest erection of my life. We all had sex with each other and then, like most women I had sex with back then, they left.

I remember that Becca had broken up with someone. Chloe was the more free-spirited one. It is so strange that I have no memory of Nellie at all while this night lived vividly with me for years to come. I have often masturbated to the memory of these two women. It was a strange serendipity that now allowed them to be in front of me after all this time.

I walk into the bar and watch them closely. I lean against a wall at the back of the room and watch my younger self dancing like an idiot. I hate myself during this drunken era so much. I am directionless and I don't even care. I hate that this person ignored his life. I hate that I failed at University, which ultimately prevented me from rising beyond the rank of a plumber. My life was ruined through the choices I made right here. I don't regret any of the sexual conquests or the fact that I have a threesome here tonight but I hate that my life's goal became drinking and sex to the point where I lost the bigger picture.

Sometimes I would ask Sam to have a threesome with me but she wasn't into it. She thought that if I had another woman there that I would fall for them. Sam told me that if I wanted to have sex with someone else I should just break up with her. I never cheated on Sam but during that seemingly endless pregnancy I definitely wanted to.

The girls from my threesome look younger than I remember. Maybe I just feel older or because more time has passed since the first time this moment happened. It's harder to track when time is folded over again and again. Becca looks less interested than I remember. She keeps looking at her phone and drinking her drink.

Chloe must be the instigator. She has selected my younger self from all of the possible candidates present. I wonder why I was chosen that night?   I look around the room and see no one stands out as a better option. It's getting late and I can only assume I was the best of the boys that were left. Chloe keeps nudging Becca and telling her to smile. She gets two shots of alcohol and almost force-feeds Becca both of them in quick succession. Chloe then orders two more for herself. Becca looks like she wants to go home but her friend seems heart set on making a memory here tonight.   I admire Chloe for her resilience in that moment. My younger self will spend years enjoying thinking about the two of them. They will become so much more beautiful and seductive to him as time passes.

They approach young Ben on the dance floor and he immediately starts sweet talking them. Ben focuses on Chloe and gets in very close to speak over the music. Becca is cautious and stares daggers. I move around the room to avoid looking too creepy.

I watch Ben smile and win Chloe over. She's smitten. Ben goes to the bathroom and the girls wait patiently.

I have similar facial hair to my past self.

We look so similar at this moment that I feel like tonight is fate.

I have to go for it.

I swoop in without a second thought and tap Chloe on the shoulder. I smile and try to act as intoxicated as I can.

'Did you change your shirt?' she asks.

'Yeah I saw it and I liked it better.' The adlib works.

I mentally pat myself on the back. Chloe starts touching the collar.

'I like it better too. Can we go?'

I lead her towards the door. They don't recognise that I'm older so maybe I've aged better than I think.

It's working.

I'm going to steal this moment from myself and live it all over again.
I put my arm around Chloe and kiss her. Becca walks just behind. We hail
a taxi and I scan the bar for my younger self while I open the door for the
girls. He looks outside and sees Becca shuffling into her seat next to
Chloe.

Ben looks directly at me.

He's seen the girls leave with me and he's confused. He's saying
something but I can't tell what it is. I get in the car and we drive away into
the night.

I don't have the keys to my Uni residence and I don't have a place in
this time. It's not a great idea to try and go back to one of their houses so I
tell the driver to take us to a hotel.

'Why are you at a hotel?' Becca asks suspiciously.

'My ceiling has a mould problem and my landlord put me up in a
hotel while they fix it.'

I kiss Chloe again and think about Nellie in the back of that taxi. The
image of her breast in Ben's mouth has burned itself into my mind. Some
things are less forgettable the second time around. I try and engage Becca.
I drop a hand onto her knee. I'll need her to participate if I want to have
this threesome again.

'I heard your boyfriend broke up with you.'

'*I'm* the one that told you that,' Becca says folding her arms over her
breasts.

'Yeah…that sucks.'

'Yeah thanks.'

'You're really hot and it's really his loss you know?' I say as kindly
as I can.

'Yeah he was a tool anyway.'

'A complete shithead!' yells Chloe.

'Fuck that guy. You're free!' I say joining in.

Becca half smiles and I give her a nudge.

It's working.

At the hotel I tell them I've lost my card and head to the reception desk alone. I check in with my Brad Dumas identification and I'm careful not to let the girls see it. They think I'm Ben and if they hear my name is Brad I'm afraid they'll smell a rat. I pay with cash and give a generous tip. We head into the assigned room and move straight to the bed. In my memory of this moment I start with Chloe and then Becca gets encouraged to join in. If I play this right after the initial awkwardness we will wind up having a fantastic sex filled evening.

Chloe straddles me on the bed and starts to dry hump me. I look over at Becca while I kiss Chloe.

'What?' she says forcing me to overt my eyes back to Chloe.

'Is your friend okay?' I say quietly. I feel like I need Chloe to help me make this happen.

Selfishly I realise that I don't want to have sex with only one of them.

'Yeah she'll be okay. Even though we agree he was an arsehole she's still not over her ex.'

'Do you think she might want to join us?'

Chloe smiles a cheeky smile that tells me everything. She has been planning for this to be a threesome all along and now two of the three people are on the same page.

'C'mon Becca... come over here,' Chloe says while she kisses down my stomach. Seconds later my testicles become like stress balls in her hands. The way she's pressing her thumb around makes me clench my fists in a mixture of pleasure and pain.

I stand up and remove my pants completely. I remember Becca liked the look of my penis last time. It's a power play that I hope will pay off.

Her eyes are fixed on my crotch. Chloe crawls over and holds my dick with both hands.

'Come *here* Becca,' she commands.

Becca silently moves over and stands near us. She keeps looking at me and then down to Chloe. She seems to have mellowed since my pants have come off.

'I'm sorry I keep staring,' Becca says.

'That's okay, I'm comfortable,' I say and take her hand in mine.

'I've never seen one that *big* before.'

The power play has worked. I somehow have the upper hand even though I'm the most exposed one in the room.

Becca doesn't move. Chloe takes her friends hand and places it on my dick.

'You need to get over that arsehole,' Chloe says as their hands meet. 'Have some fun.'

They start to kiss each other, slowly at first and then more furiously. I feel like once again I am the luckiest man in the world. This was such a thrill the first time around. Chloe and Becca turn and look at me, cheeks still touching. I smile as they both take turns putting me in their mouths. I try and control myself but it feels so good. To the surprise of all three of us it takes less than a minute before I've finished.

I couldn't help myself.

Chloe and Becca are angry to say the least. Their faces are now partially covered in semen and the evening is ruined.

'You're such a creep!' Becca yells while trying to clean up.

'What the hell *loser*…' Chloe says as she stands up.

They both start to laugh and point at me.

'What a fucking arsehole!' Becca says as she grabs her handbag from the floor.

'Fuck you,' I reply, wiping myself with my un-gloved left hand.

'You might have a big dick but you're a biiiiiig disappointment. Go fuck *yourself* next time.'

The girls leave with a chorus of mockery as I try my best to clean myself up.

I stole this experience from myself and then fucked it up. Suddenly I feel myself slipping into a depression that I haven't experienced in years.

I am back in Australia with a renewed purpose. In order to find my parents I break into the orphanage where I grew up. Everything is the same as it was when I was a child because technically I *am* a child at this point in time and everything *is* exactly as it was. It's like walking through a vivid dream. I take a moment to roam the corridors of my youth. Everything seems so small and simple. The world was smaller then. I find myself sitting on the floor and staring at nothing. The carpet feels familiar.

I've come so far since my time here.

I've been all over the world and had a secret life that most would envy if they knew the particulars. But ultimately it's been a highlight show for just one person. It's hard to imagine that soon I'll erase all of it, and then myself.

Was it worth it?

Would it have mattered if I'd just come straight here and ended it all? I guess I just wasn't ready for it to be over yet.

I am now.

I sleep for a while on the carpet but soon I'm startled by footsteps. I see a security guard with a torch through the window. He's most likely investigating my breaking and entering. I hold him at knifepoint and make him give me all the access keys I will require before pulsing back to use them. I'm becoming reckless with my pulses now that I don't care anymore. I have no reason to live, just like my aging son from the future.

I find my personal records in an office that I'd never been into before. They are fairly basic forms with some redacted information.

And then the revelation I've wanted my whole life happens out of nowhere. My parents' names are Harry Preston and Linda Kellerman.

Harry Preston and Linda Kellerman.

I am Ben Preston.

Or Ben Kellerman.

It's so strange to put names to these identities that have loomed in my mind for so long. It's even stranger to be alone in a dark office when I learn these elusive names. I lick my dry lips as I hold my birth certificate. The fact that they have different last names piques my interest. Maybe they were young and spent a single night together. Maybe they weren't ready and that's why they gave me up.

There is a street address but when I check it out no one there knows my parents. After further investigation I'm disappointed to find their graves. They were buried side by side in a dual funeral plot in the corner of a small cemetery next to a main road. It's a depressing sight. I'd been visiting graveyards like this randomly for years. There is no mention of me on their headstones either.

According to the engraving they died three days after I was born. This gives me a small window in my timeline to find them, decide which of them to give the glove to and then disappear. The scary thought that creeps into my mind is whether I'll make the right choice.

Will it matter?

Perhaps not in the scheme of things.

Jack knew he had to give the glove to me because Sam was going to die. But both my parents die three days after I'm born. I might have to save them the same way I saved Lola.

I am the only person alive that ever saw Old Jack, and now my parents might be the only ones who will remember me.

It's so backwards.

I might not be able to convince them that any of this is even real. Maybe the coins I'm carrying from the future will be enough? Maybe not. For years I have wondered about the purpose of the glove and why my distant relatives started this. While I may never know the answer what I have realised is that I've been selfishly using the glove and that needs to stop.

Harry Preston and Linda Kellerman.

My mind goes into overdrive. Why *do* they have different last names? Maybe they had intended to marry but died before they could. Was I the result of some horrible event like a rape? I shudder at the thought.

When I've got myself ready I head back to the day after their deaths. I infiltrate the morgue and pay off an employee for information on my parents. They were found dead together in the Hyatt Hotel but the details are sketchy. There are no bruises or wounds on either of them. No one will be doing an autopsy for a few days and though my new friend offers to show me the bodies I can't bring myself to look at them. I don't want the first time I see my parents to be in this horrible place.

Somewhere baby Ben is crying uncontrollably for his mother.

I speak to employees at the Hyatt Hotel but nobody will spill the beans to me. All I find out is that it happened in Room 202 on the second floor.

My parents died there.

I think back but I'm not sure I've ever stayed on the second floor of a Hyatt Hotel in my time pulsing around. The hotel Managers have asked their staff not to talk to the press. In a way I'm reassured by all of this. The reason my parents never tried to find me was because they were dead. My parents wanted me after all! I would have been too young to deal with it so the blanket explanation I always got was that I had been given up for adoption and the details were sealed. Maybe the various foster families knew that Harry and Linda were dead. Maybe they never knew. *Chinese*

Whispers across generations. I stopped asking at a young age and by the time I wanted to know it felt like too little too late.

I pulse back through time with more nervous tension than ever before.

This time I will save them.

I check into the Hyatt and request Room 200. Suddenly I'm pacing the carpet in the room adjacent to theirs. I eat all my meals inside the hotel using the room service menu. My mind races at the thought of meeting my parents for the first time. I hear them arrive through the walls the day they check in – two days after my birth. I listen for their movements but neither of them leaves the room.

There is no shouting or fighting.

I stay awake all night but my parents remain silent. At some unknown hour of the night due to accumulated fatigue I regrettably succumb to sleep.

In the morning there is a commotion outside my door and I head into the corridor to find a maid knocking on the door of Room 202. A male employee knocks even harder but neither Linda nor Harry responds. The employee tells me to go back to my room but I stand firm. The maid steps back and the man kicks the door in with all of his might.

When the door crashes down a cloud of gas hits all three of us in the face. I'm overcome and for a moment I can't breathe. I push through my initial shock and see both Harry and Linda lying on the living room floor next to a broken gas pipe.

They are dead.

I don't want to stay in the room for a minute longer than I need to.

I have to go back and fix this. They don't deserve to die like that. I leave the hotel, pulse back to two days after my birth and check in again. This time I spend some money on a nice suit and get my hair cut. Harry and Linda check in and I wait until the evening of their deaths to knock on their door. When Harry opens the door the first thing I notice is that we are the same height.

'Can I help you?' he asks with searching eyes.

'Hi there… sorry to interrupt your stay. I've been informed that there is a potential gas leak on this floor and I'm checking all the rooms. Would you mind if I come in?'

'Yes I mind. My wife and I just want to be left alone.'

Interesting that he refers to her as his wife considering the different last names.

'Sir, it's vital that you-'

'-LEAVE US BE!' Harry yells at me before slamming the door.

My father just yelled at me for the first time.

I knock again and when he doesn't open the door I shout through it.

'Listen to me, I know you might think it's safe but it's my job to inspect the pipes.'

Silence.

I knock again but they don't answer. It takes the all too familiar smell of gas hitting me in the face to realise what's going on. I start charging my shoulder into the door.

'Harry?' I yell in desperation.

I can't let them die.

The wooden door starts to give way against the determination of my movements. It takes a run-up and bashing my shoulder with all my strength to finally get into the room. I collapse through the half attached door and spill onto the carpet inside. The smell is overwhelming and my biological mother is unconscious next to the broken gas pipe. Harry stares me down with eyes of stone.

'You idiot,' he says, red in the face. 'You've ruined everything.'

I try to grab his arm but he shakes me loose.

'We have to get out of here,' I plead.

'No! Don't you understand? We *want* to die.'

The gas is starting to make me dizzy. Harry pulls out a gun and raises it to his temple. Everything happens in slow motion.

His eyes become wild.

He's going to shoot himself.

I can't watch.

I activate the glove and flee before I'm forced to watch my father kill himself.

Before I can see Lola again there is an event I need to attend on my way backwards through time. I've heard all about today from Nathan.

Today is the day he marries Lana.

He's told me in the past that marrying her was the best day of his life. It's the culmination of all of his good decisions.

Becoming sober.

Choosing Lana instead of his rock and roll lifestyle.

The guests arrive at the boat club in droves. A blackboard near the door points guests out toward the water. I remove my sunglasses and let myself be open to what's coming next. I've bought a suit for the occasion because I need to feel like I belong here. It's going to be an emotional day and I'm hoping to experience as much of it as I can.

It's perfectly cloudless with almost no breeze. The two of them have drawn a large crowd of guests as well as curious bystanders that just happen to be at the boat club today. I see Nathan first, standing with two men in the shade between two large trees. He seems calm and collected as he gladhands relatives and poses for photos. His beard is shorter today than I've ever seen it and a lot less grey.

As he waits in the shade the music hits and his bride appears. Lana is in a silky white wedding dress with make up that makes her look like a porcelain doll. I watch Nathan's face as she moves past onlookers and towards him.

I've always liked Lana and Nathan.

They've always been a representation of a solid relationship and I've always admired them from afar.

Lana stands opposite Nathan and starts to cry.

These tears don't immediately feel like happy ones.

There is a point in the ceremony where Lana excuses herself and stands crying behind one of the trees. Nathan tries to encourage her back and eventually after some awkwardness she complies.

Their vows are pleasant enough but I don't find myself feeling emotional.

It feels as though I was wrong to put their relationship on a pedestal.

A final novelty of the night is that I get to watch Nathan's band play for the first time. They had stopped playing by the time I met Nathan so all I had heard was rumours and tales from his touring days. I'm disappointed to say the least. His guitar playing is reminiscent of a dying cat while the lyrics and mostly *ooh's* and *aah's*. The crowd is extremely enthusiastic but I think they might *really* be clapping because the performance has concluded.

Towards the end of the night I creep out of the background and say hello.

'G'day… I just wanted to say congratulations,' I say while I shake Nathan's hand.

'Oh cool. Thanks man. What was your name?'

'Brad,' I say. 'I work here at the boat club.'

His eyes light up.

'Great! Did you manage to get it?'

'Sorry… get what?'

'The weed?'

I'm taken aback. Nathan told me he was clean and sober by his wedding. I can also smell alcohol on his breath.

'I thought you didn't smoke weed anymore,' I say hoping he will lower his eyebrows.

He laughs.

'Nah! That's just something you have to say…you know… to keep the in-laws happy.'

'Oh okay.'

I tell him I'm not the guy who can get him weed and he becomes dismissive of me immediately.

He's not a role model.

He's a liar.

I was wrong.

Time travel has shown me that things are never black and white.

I glance over to Lana and see her fighting back tears while getting hugged by friends and family.

This has not been the fairy tale that I was led to believe.

The two of them spend most of the night apart chatting to other guests. Nathan disappears for a while, which delays their first dance, and reappears smelling like he found his marijuana supplier after all.

I think about punching him in the face but I'm right handed and I don't want to risk damaging the glove.

He's not worth it.

After a period of rest and mental recovery I decide it is time to redeem myself. I explore my old haunts and am thrilled to find the stores and arcades intact. I play *Street Fighter* and *Daytona* for hours, losing myself in the muscle memory of my youth. I head to my University campus and find Doug first. I watch him reading underneath a tree despite the cold weather. A trail of smoke flies up from behind the book.

He's smoking weed behind there.

I watch him covertly inhale and smile knowingly to myself. I think about how successful he becomes in my future. It makes sense that his rich parents would set him up for a rich and successful life. I always envied him. It's strange to think about it as *my* future. I'll never see it unfold.

Through the act of my being here – outside of time – the future is different. I imagine what the world would be like if I walked up to Doug and shot him and then myself – removing us from this time completely. I shudder a little as I consider it because it brings back the all too fresh memory of strangling my younger self. If I was to remove the younger version of myself and then I was to die then this would become the *only* timeline. What would the future hold for Sam? There is no doubt in my mind that she would have her fair share of suitors. Sam and I were never suited to stay together in the long run. I was too immature to grow up when she became pregnant. I started spiralling and I didn't know how to stop.

Eventually young Ben turns up and shakes Doug's hand. I watch them walk to Doug's car and drive away – presumably towards *Secrets* or to smoke weed together. They are off to do nothing and waste their lives. Neither of them will amount to anything until they are free from each other. I spend some time at the campus and absorb the minutiae of the place. In my heart I know that in order to save Lola I will have to put myself in danger. I'm worried that if I am murdered saving Lola then I will have a very painful death as opposed to the death Old Jack had. The death I've been promised. Painless. A horrible death might be the death I deserve though, which scares me even more. I watch oblivious students hurry to class and the wind blow through the tall trees. A redhead smiles at me as she passes and for the briefest of moments I consider following her. She looks cold as she hurries away.

I smile a sad smile. These kind of indulgent moments are over for me. I can't just pursue any random girl that I see.

Lola is my destiny.

I have spent many nights wondering how she died. At this moment in time I know she is still alive and I solidify my mission to keep it that way. I say farewell to my institution of higher learning and head off to see Lola. I assume she'll be out in the world as it's the middle of the day so I take my time and walk. The city feels more peaceful than I remember. Maybe I never took the time to stop and look around the first time I was here. I was busy studying – for a while anyway.

When I get to Lola's place it looks smaller than I remember but the brown fence and bright green door are exactly the same. It's like I'm walking through one of her paintings. It looks like she's not home so I walk around and check out the neighbourhood. It's not a particularly clean or safe looking place to live and the area won't be gentrified for years so I try to keep my wits about me. The population is a mix of ethnicities and they seem to clash on some unspoken level. I feel the heat of each person staring.

Do I stand out that much?

I hide the glove in my pocket. I buy an overcoat in a local store to fight off the cold air. The cashier seems annoyed that he has to serve me. I'm uncomfortable here. I consider getting a place nearby and studying the area but I don't know if I have the patience. Maybe I'll get my own place to live next time I pulse back. All I can think about is Lola's face and how I'm going to save her. I want to take her away from this cesspool.

At around dusk my patience is rewarded. Lola carries two clear shopping bags to her door and puts them down while she digs her keys out from her pocket. I only watch her for a minute or so before she walks through the door but it's enough.

Lola is the reason time travel was invented.

I'm sure of it. This is the culmination of my life. I will save her and give her the life that was stolen away. It is love at first sight all over again. I head to the nicest hotel I can find. It's adequate but it reminds me I'm definitely still on the wrong side of the tracks. I drag the side table in front of the front door like a paranoid idiot and fall sleep for a long time.

When I wake up I'm dying of thirst. One practical issue with ongoing time travel is that you forget to eat and drink at regular intervals because of how irregular they are for you. It's late so I shower and head to *Secrets* hoping to find Lola working. A wave of nostalgia hits me the moment I walk inside. The place is exactly as I remember. The club is fairly empty which means every half naked girl offers me a private dance. I politely decline and order a drink. I am quietly thankful that Ben and Doug aren't here.

'I'll have a double scotch please.'

'Great order!' says the bartender happily to me. 'That's my drink when I'm off duty too!'

I give him a healthy tip and he gives me the thumbs up. I leave the drink on the bar as an exercise of self-control. I don't need to drink it and this makes me happy. The counter is only marginally stickier than the floor. I start to imagine what percentage of it is semen as I make my way to the back of the room. I'll avoid all surfaces from now on. I see some girls that look familiar but I guess none of them ever left an impression like Lola did. I don't want anyone else to catch my eye anymore. The idea that I could one day be with Lola has given me tunnel vision.

Lola doesn't show up so after an hour I head upstairs to the brothel. The purple walls seem new. I pay for a blonde and tell her I only want to talk.

'We can do anything you like handsome.'

'I was wondering if you know Lola?'

'I know a lot of ladies. Did you want to have a threesome? That could be fun.'

'I've had a threesome thanks.'

'That's sexy. Tell me about it.'

I think back to my short-lived evening with Becca and Chloe. I remember their laughing and mocking the second time around and decide not to share.

'I'd rather talk about Lola. She works downstairs in the strip club sometimes.'

'Lola. Blonde?'

'That's right.'

'Sure I know her,' she says, as she gets comfortable in a chair. 'I might need some help remembering though.'

I give her five hundred dollars and after I convince her I'm not involved with any kind of law enforcement she asks me what I want to know.

'What's her real name?'

'Helena. I don't know her last name.'

Helena.

The name suits her.

'Tell me about her. What does Helena like?'

'She's an artist. Maybe you could buy her some new paints. Personally I like chocolates.'

Lola… *Helena*… painted the tiger with the peacock in its mouth that hung over the bed when we first made love. That image has been burnt into my memory. She must be an amazing artist. I silently hope that I live to see more of her work.

'Do you want to fool around at all? It might be good practice for Lola,' the blonde offers trying to upsell me.

'No thank you.'

'You sure?' she asks as she opens her blouse and squeezes her nipples between her fingers.

'I'm not interested.'

She puts her breasts away but continues her campaign.

'I won't charge you for it. I just kind of want to fuck you.'

'Why?'

'Well, you're really into Helena, or Lola or whatever you want to call her. You're here asking all about her. I kind of want you because you want her I guess.'

'That's sort of fucked up.'

'I know right? I think I have intimacy issues. That might explain why I'm a prostitute, hey?'

She laughs maniacally and I excuse myself.

The next day while scoping out her place I see the mailman drop letters into Lola's letterbox. I wait for the street to clear and then I head to the mailbox and check the mail.

Helena Volodin.

Lola's real name *is* Helena. It makes me think of Helen of Troy. Helena has a face that would launch a thousand ships too. I smile to myself and put her mail back.

I follow Helena to and from work without suspicion. She sometimes meets women at shops or cafes. I never recognise any of them from the club but I can't be sure. She buys painting supplies and groceries often. I rent out an apartment across the road from her. I buy a camera with a decent lens. My documentation of her life becomes obsessive. I watch her paint on nights when she is at home and feeling restless. I can never see what she is painting from my angle. Is she painting the tiger with the peacock in its mouth? What does it mean to her? I have never seen any of her other paintings. Does she just love tigers and hate peacocks?

Helena rarely has visitors but her phone rings a lot. It seems there is no one in her life romantically but she is not short of admirers. Men sometimes stare at her in the street. I can't blame them. When I first met the woman I knew as Lola it changed me. After I lost my virginity I became a more confident man. Having spent all this time watching Helena I think of her as a different person to the Lola I knew. She looks the same but she is now more three-dimensional. I have spent a lot more time mentally checking Helena for clues and getting to know her habits. This woman is new and pure. I see her as my salvation.

I watch her paint her toenails and laugh. I imagine her drawing tiny faces on each one. One morning I watch her cut her own hair. Helena is captivating. I see her sashay around in her space happily.

Ignorance is certainly bliss.

Only I know this woman is doomed.

One day soon Helena will be murdered. I now firmly believe that this is the reason I have been given this glove. I *must* save her. Maybe her children are important. Maybe *our* children are important to humanity. Helena has become the most important person in my world. I am her guardian angel and I will not let her die.

Time rolls forward and I become comfortable in my new apartment. It's small but it has an amazing view. I don't miss travelling through time. I enjoy the regularity of my new life here. I have a corner of the room dedicated to exercise, which I perform regularly.

I don't own a TV or a radio but I did purchase a king-sized mattress and a second hand desk to sit at as I monitor the building. I was able to procure a very cheap blue car that I assume I'll need to follow her from time to time.

I'm prepared.

I read books and keep track of lottery draws in a notepad. I'll need them for the next time I pulse back. I meditate regularly and find myself calmer than I've ever been. I feel rested. My mission this time is purely observational.

I need to know what happened.

Sometimes Helena leaves her curtains open for a cold breeze on a hot night. It feels creepy watching Helena change clothes or shower. I have tried to stop myself but I occasionally see her naked. I have also learned that she likes to masturbate before bed, which I never watch. The first time she started to do it I turned bright red. I now know I am watching someone that doesn't know she is being watched. These moments are supposed to be intimate and private. I would not want someone to watch me like that.   I try to be as respectful as possible. As time goes on I learn restraint.

I admire Helena from afar.

I love her.

Helena never really looks up at me. Sometimes I want her to but she never does. She doesn't talk to the neighbours. There is a middle-aged man in glasses that is almost stalking her as well as I am. I note all his movements in case he turns out to be the killer. She is still a mystery to me. I think about trying to source listening devices but part of me doesn't want to know everything. I'm enjoying getting to know her one day at a time.

One night I fall asleep at my desk facing her window. I wake up, spin around, and see two men from *Secrets* knocking on her door loudly. It's four in the morning. They look like greasy haired bikers from afar. The leather jackets are a major clue. They yell in Russian but there is no response. Maybe I need to learn Russian. The lights are off at Helena's place and eventually the men leave in a black car.

I stay awake until morning and watch Helena peer out of her window. She was in there the whole time but stayed quiet. What was going on? I think back to the porn set that I saw once at *Secrets*. I silently hope she's not involved. This solidifies to me again that Helena deserves a better life than the one she has. The one she will soon lose.

I consider following the men. I want to discover why they were at Helena's place but I'm afraid to leave her alone. I have to keep my eyes on the target in case something happens. One night I'm following Helena at work and I see her get in the car with a man.

It's me.

I follow Ben as he drives Doug's station wagon back to Helena's place.   I let them go inside together before heading up to my bedroom across the road. She won't be killed tonight because tonight was *our* night. The night I lost my virginity.

I watch my younger self closely through the lens of my camera and it all comes back to me. I am so jealous of myself. He looks nervous as he shifts his weight around in her living room. I remember saving her from some uncouth thug at *Secrets* and driving her home. I remember I was mad at Doug for some reason but I can't remember the details.

Everything was different after Lola.

My view is obscured and I can only make out a portion of the room. I see myself for only a few seconds at a time. Suddenly a metal bin is knocked over down the street and I jump. My senses are in overdrive. A drunk in a suit is stumbling down the road. I watch him walk up to Doug's station wagon and whip out his penis. He takes a piss on the driver's side door and continues on his way.

When I return to the windows I can only see the end of the sofa where Ben is sleeping. I wait until the middle of the night hoping to relive this again as a voyeur. This is different to watching her masturbate because I was there. I have ownership over this experience. Eventually Lola hovers into view with something in her hand. It must be the Viagra in water.

She made me feel like the best lover in the world because she chemically guaranteed that I would be good at it. I don't remember how long I lasted the first time but it couldn't have been long. In my memory we fucked for hours.

I watch with fascination as Ben loses his virginity. It's a surreal experience for me this time around as I can only imagine what he and Lola are doing. I still don't have a clear view. I tell myself that it's Lola and not Helena in that room. Lola belongs in my past – with Ben. Helena is my future.

I can separate them for now the same way I separate this version of myself from my past.

As I sit in the dark I remember the time I tried to steal Jessica from Doug. It wasn't authentic. I think about the time I 'stole' the threesome from myself. It was different the second time around. I can't replicate things and relive my life that way anymore. For one thing I look so much older that it would impact the way Lola looked at me. She might not trust me in the same way she did with my younger self. I'd only make things worse. If I intercepted this night from Ben I would only ruin it and besmirch the memory just like I did with Chloe and Becca.

It needs to stay in my past.

My plan to change my identity took a long time. I started by going to the casino and watching people play roulette. I would then pulse back and win a bunch of money. It was easy to remember the results as I'd only just seen them. I made sure to only bet a few times so as not to draw any unwanted attention. I checked into the same lush hotel suite as Old Jack. I ordered food, watched movies and had prostitutes delivered to my door.

Every time I travelled back in time I had to carry money in my pockets so I would have it again when I went back. Each time I had to check into the same hotel all over again.

It was amazing to live life with no responsibilities. If I was hungry I ate and if I was horny I fucked someone. I was actively following all my most primitive programming. Whatever I wanted, I got. I was on holiday from my life. Eventually I changed my name to Brad Dumas. 'Brad' was close enough to Ben that I would be able to evolve to it organically, and 'Dumas' in honour of my favourite Author Alexander Dumas – who wrote *The Count of Monte Cristo*. I was now just like the lead character Edmond. I had reinvented myself as an important and powerful figure thanks to my good fortune. I had no revenge to seek but I was concocting a plan for my immediate future.

The glove will one day take me back to see Lola. I need to find out what happened to her. I can save her and prevent her death. Then I can be with her and finally be happy. I know that when I'm ready eventually I'll have to go back and find my parents. I'll have to choose one of them and give them the glove. I'll have to teach them to use it and then I'll cease to be.

Knowing all of these events are safely waiting for me in my past is what allows me to enjoy myself now. I've decided to live my life as loudly as I can, knowing that it all ends with my birth. It is still scary to me so I will use the glove sparingly. It's very disorientating too. Each time I go back it's closer to the end. I'll have to take better care of myself. There's no limit to what I can do as long as I don't die before I do it. The air tastes better somehow now.

Brad Dumas is a happy man.

I decide to win the lottery. I watch the draw and note the numbers. I line my pockets with cash and take myself to a local park bench. I figure it doesn't make sense to pulse back from a hotel room because there might be someone else staying there when I reappear. I go back to the default minute before my last visit and wait. I check into a hotel again. I have to wait a couple of weeks to catch up to the night of lotto draw. It feels like wasted time. I decide that when I have twenty million dollars I will travel.

There is nothing for me here.

I get the money with relative ease and charter a private jet. I travel to Europe and visit worlds I never thought I would see in person. I'm careful not to draw attention to myself. Some people question my gloved hand and I find myself offering the same explanation as Old Jack.

'I was burnt in an accident.'

It always elicits a sympathetic reaction. I treat the world like a stage. I walk around knowing that I am merely a spectator and that if I choose to I can manipulate things. In my travels I find myself visiting the wonders of the world. Sam, Vladimir and my plumbing job are forgotten among the beauty of the places I see.

I meet other nomads like myself on their own journeys across the globe.   I read allegedly important works of literature and find myself becoming philosophical about the meaning of life and the nature of being. I'm lonely sometimes because in truth I am the only one in the world that knows what's going to happen. I watch television and see terrorists killing themselves and taking hundreds along with them. I watch natural disasters wipe out villages. I sit by and see school shootings, disease, poverty and death. I'm like an impotent Superman. I can't change any of it.

It's been months since I've used the glove. If I choose to go back now to stop a crime before it's been committed then I'll have to sit around for months waiting for the day I know it will happen. Then I have to hope I can actually stop it without being killed myself.

It's far too dangerous.

If I die then I never have children. If I never have children then down the line my ancestors don't create the glove. It would all end with me. If I'm buried with the glove presumably it will decompose over time and the gift of time travel dies with me. Unless my parallel self has the kid I was supposed to have. Old Jack. But Jack will never exist so long as I keep travelling backwards. Am I just a cog in a much bigger machine? I feel like the only responsibility I have is to continue on this path. I feel obliged to ensure the glove is passed on.

The only crime I want to stop is whatever random act of violence kills Lola. When I get back there I will be with her and then, after our happy life together, when I'm ready to say goodbye to her I'll find my family. That's a long way down the line though. I want to enjoy my final days of bachelorhood. Lola is my destiny. I'll settle down with her and have the life I should have had the first time around.

I don't want to source a gun for protection. If I get into trouble I'd probably just run away and if it was serious I could always click my fingers together and escape. It does weigh on me that each time I use the glove I'm getting closer to the end, so I want to avoid using it as much as possible.

The pulses reset everything but happily I keep my memories. I spend months in France and almost a year exploring Italy. I make temporary friends and sleep with hundreds of women along the way. I'm careful to use protection each time. Now that I have time I consider all kinds of insane possibilities. What if I have sex with someone and *they* have my child? When that child is born, unbeknownst to me, they could come back from a future where my ancestors *still* create the time travelling glove. What if my child gives that glove to their mother instead of me? The moment the mother time travels back I would cease to exist. They would send a pulse that would wipe me out just like Old Jack. There would be a version of me somewhere out there, probably with Sam, but *I* wouldn't be here anymore. Only one glove can exist at a time. I hope I'm wrong. I hope existing *outside of time* means I'll remain. But I can't take that chance. Life has become too valuable to me. I can't risk these kinds of hypothetical scenarios.

I go to cultural events like the running of the bulls in Spain. I don't run personally but it is a spectacle I'll never forget. I can never participate in anything that might result in my death or serious injury. I smoke in Amsterdam and decide to stay there for almost six months. After that I see castles, vineyards, The Parthenon, search for Loch Ness, see amazing works of art and eat in five star restaurants. I see Buckingham Palace, walk across Abbey Road, watch live music and visit historical sites.

As a species we seem destined to wipe ourselves out. We build bombs; we fight each other and destroy the Earth's natural resources. With time to reflect I feel great sorrow for the human race. We don't deserve to live here. I hope that the glove will course correct the mistakes of our species.

In America I rent a car and drive from the West Coast of Los Angeles through to New York on the East Coast. It takes months but I stop everywhere and do everything I can think of. With each place I go there is a sense that it will be the last time I am there. There is too much of the world to see and I wont have the time to repeat myself and retrace my steps. I linger in San Francisco, go native in Texas and immerse myself in Graceland.

The world is made small through my conquering of her.

In the evenings I can almost always find someone to share my bed. I spend time courting and seducing women everywhere I go. My appetite for flesh increases and soon I feel the familiar pull from my days of addiction.

The truth that I now face is that I have become a sex addict once more. The need is now so great that I have live-in prostitutes at my beck and call. I fuck multiple women at once in every conceivable way. I tear through every position in the Kama Sutra until I feel empty and more alone than ever. I increase the number of women, whom I line up in more and more degrading ways. I experiment with orgies and then try men. I sample everything that is legal and blur the lines constantly. I'm completely insatiable. I feel like I'm above everyone. I exist outside of time and therefore my actions do not need justification.

I turn on the television and see a beautiful woman in a commercial. I hire someone to find out who she is and where I can find her. I introduce myself to everyone as Brad Dumas and appeal to the things they desire most. I have money; I can offer them a better life. I calculate what they need and then I am rewarded. Sometimes someone will intrigue me. I'll stalk them and pulse over and over again until I become bored of them. They offer themselves to me and I chew them up and spit them out again. I have become a violent lover and there are few that walk away from me without a mark on their body.

The marks will vanish when I'm done.

It will be as though it never happened.

Some love it and beg me for more. If I become bored with my surroundings or my company I move on. I travel for years and never give a second thought to anyone other that myself. The glove becomes like an extension of my hand.

Of my identity.

Of me.

I want to wear it forever.

Doug wants to go on a double date. It's a true testament to how much we've grown up that I'm happy to oblige. Sam is keen and apparently so is Jessica. It's a Tuesday night so the plan is a simple dinner at an Italian place, although if everyone gets along maybe we'll go out for dessert or something after.

We have also received an invitation to their wedding in the mail. Sam is thrilled to learn the wedding will be at the beach an hour from our place. She is so excited that she joins me in the shower.

'Honey…'

'Yeah?' I reply with hair full of shampoo.

'Do you think we could stay at the beach for a day or two after the wedding?'

Sam starts stroking my butt.

'Well, we're only an hour away.'

'But…' she smiles and pauses, 'if we stay there it will *feel* like a holiday.'

She moves her hand from my butt to my thigh. It's very effective and I quickly rinse the shampoo away. Sam gives me a quick kiss.

'What do you think?' she asks with wide eyes.

'Ok.'

Looking back on it now I can see I was played. Sam exchanged sex for a holiday. The bed and breakfast does looks like fun though. Each room is decorated in the style of a different rock star so it's a bit of a novelty.

Doug texts me in advance of the dinner and tells me he will pay and that we should only bring our appetites. Money had always been an issue between us in the past and now I feel like we're right back at University. I decide not to fight him on this.

Jessica Nash is an elegant woman who seems like she belongs in the Royal Family. She has such an intimidating aura that Sam and I find ourselves fascinated by everything she says.

'Douglas and I met at a café. It was so sweet,' Jessica tells us while she holds Doug's hand.

Douglas?

'She was reading Great Expectations and I sat with her and had a drink,' Doug continues in a practiced manner.

'We had an iced tea and the rest is history really,' she concludes with a quick kiss to Doug's cheek.

'That's sweet. And are you excited about the wedding?' Sam asks with a smile.

Jessica seems to light up at the question. She tells us about the cake and the difficulty in seating her family. She is measured and witty. I lean back and watch Sam and Jessica interact. I can't help but compare them. Am I jealous? Why do I want Jessica all of a sudden?

Maybe it's the idea of someone new.

Maybe it's because she's with Doug.

I try not to stare but I make calculated glances at her body throughout the meal.

'Doug is going to make such a good father. Look at those eyes!'

I'd never really looked at Doug's eyes closely before. They were okay I guess. Since when did good eyes equate to good parenting?

Jessica and Doug order the same chicken dish. I order a pizza while Sam orders gnocchi. Sam then proceeds to eat three slices of my dinner. I consider ordering more as Doug has agreed to pay but feel a little awkward about it.

'So I hear that you did a criminology degree Ben, is that right?' Jessica asks.

'Oh… uh yeah. I was studying that when I went to University with Doug but I dropped out.'

'Why was that?'

'Well, I decided that I wasn't happy doing criminology after all.'

'So what do you do now?' Jessica enquires as she props her head up with one hand.

'I'm a plumber.'

There is a moment of silence as Jessica nods and tries to think of a follow up question.

'Someone's gotta do it!' Sam says with a laugh.

Jessica has a sip of wine. I decide to elaborate.

'I had a drinking problem that really damaged my grades. I went out a lot. Sometimes every night of the week. I wasn't in a good headspace and it was all too much for me. I wasn't ready to study.'

'Oh I see,' says Jessica sympathetically. 'Do you think you will go back and finish your degree now then?'

'No… probably not. I don't like the idea of being a mature aged student.'

'I see. I see.'

I wish she'd stop saying that.

'I mean… my boss Vladimir doesn't really know all that much about plumbing so I'm kind of the boss now… unofficially. So I guess in the near future I'll be the boss *officially*.'

As I said it out loud it sounds like a terrible career plan. Hope against hope that your boss will go away and let you be in charge.

'Sam runs a catering business,' I say deflecting.

Sam drives the conversation for a while and I have a moment to think. I look at my friend Doug. He's grown up a lot since those University days. I am definitely jealous but it's not *just* because of Jessica.

He's got it together and I don't.

I don't know if I can marry Sam.

Can I be faithful to her forever?

Do I *want* to be?

I don't know if I can be a plumber forever. I start to feel depressed about my future.

They look so happy. Do *we* look happy to them? I can't imagine we do.

They certainly look more at ease tonight.

I feel anxious about everything right now.

Later that night as I have sex with Sam I close my eyes and pretend that she's Jessica. Then as I climax I find myself remembering my night with Lola.

I lie awake trying to imagine the easiest way out of my engagement to Sam.

I can't marry her.

Helena is getting dressed up and I don't know why. She is wearing bright red lipstick and a long dark brown trench coat. I watch her in between bites of my dinner from my window and think about our conversation. When she died the first time around it remained unsolved. Maybe nobody cared because she was an immigrant. I'm glad I'm here to make sure both of us get a second chance.

Helena starts walking as the sunset steals across the sky. It is magic hour and the trees are lit up with licks of orange. She is carrying an umbrella, which makes me check the sky again. Does she know something I don't?   I haven't owned an umbrella in a long time. I can remember a few moments where the rain annoyed me and I simply pulsed away to nicer weather. I've become spoilt like that. I snap my fingers and the seasons change. I stay about twenty feet behind her and scan the horizon for potential danger. Her warm breath swirls past her head as she picks up speed. My hours of training have kept me physically ready for whatever happens next.

I silently imagine we are walking together arm in arm. I watch the neighbourhood fold into their houses as they cold intensifies. It's dark now and Helena has been reduced to a silhouette. Where is she going at this hour? Maybe I spooked her when I told her someone was trying to kill her. This might be my fault. I should have just let her death play out so I knew exactly what was going to happen. My interference has made Helena jumpy.

As we start to head downhill a van driving towards us slows down. One of the goons from the park puts his hand out the window and fires two shots at Helena. It's calculated and gives me no time at all to react.

She falls to the pavement as they stop. They pick her body up at either-end and start to put her into the van.

'Hey!' I yell at the top of my lungs.

Without a word the thug with the gun starts shooting at me. Two shots.   I dive behind a parked car and check myself. He's missed me. I crawl underneath for cover.

'I've called the police!' I call out. 'They're on their way!'

I watch from my vantage point underneath the car. The two men casually get into their vehicle and drive away. They make murder look like a hobby. I wait until I can't hear them anymore before I get up and leave the safety of my barricade. I remember that Helena's body was discovered at the docks last time. I can assume that these men were going to take her there and dump her body for a fisherman to discover. I run over to her and brush the hair out of her eyes. She's barely breathing.

'Helena? Stay with me.'

There is blood on my glove now.

She's dying right in front of my eyes.

'How…did…' she says between laboured breaths.

'It's going to be alright. I'm going to fix this.'

She clutches my hand tightly. She looks so afraid. Her eyes are glassy as she breathes for the final time and dies in my arms. Even though I knew this moment was coming it was impossible for me to stop.

I've learned that I need to be more careful.

I can't save Helena if I'm dead.

And I *must* save her next time.

I approach Harry alone in the lobby after he's checked in and pretend to stick a gun into his back.

'Don't move,' I say as I scan the room for Linda.

'I don't have any money,' he says calmly.

'Where is Linda Kellerman?' I say as I jab my finger into his side.

Harry half turns and raises his eyebrow at me.

'She's in the bathroom throwing up blood.'

Throwing up blood?

'What are you on about?' I demand.

This is a troubling turn of events. We are almost alone except for a couple of employees behind the reception desk. They are oblivious as they answer phone calls and jot down information.

'How do you know my Linda?' he asks.

'I know her husband Michael. The man you *stole* her from,' I say.

There is no strong reaction from Harry, which makes me nervous.

'A friend of Michael's huh? Fantastic.'

'Why is she throwing up blood?'

'Because Linda is dying.'

'Dying? But she just had a baby.'

Me.

Harry squints and turns his body completely. I hide my hand behind my back to avoid letting him see I don't really have a gun. For some unknown reason I still keep my fingers in the shape of a gun behind my back. Even though we are the same height I'm suddenly shrinking on the spot as I face off against my father.

'How do you know about that?' Harry asks as he squints at me.

'I… just do.'

'Have you been *following* us?' he says menacingly.

'No.'

Yes.

'You listen to me, whoever you are, you tell Michael to stop following us. I don't want to see either of you ever again.'

Linda appears from the bathroom. She's confused and slinks over to Harry's side. Our eyes meet and she looks at me with a strange flicker of recognition. Does she realise who I am? Is some sort of maternal instinct kicking in?

Before I can speak to her Harry takes her by the arm and walks away. He isn't afraid I'm going to shoot him and he never looks back.

She's dying.

I have to speak to her.

I pulse back and wait for them to check in again. This time I watch Linda run for the bathroom as Harry waits with the bags. I use an *Out of Order* sign and close off the women's bathroom to the public.

Linda casts a lonely figure at a white porcelain sink. She is dry retching while the water runs. There are about ten stalls but none of them appear to be occupied. I approach her with caution.

'Linda?'

'Get out of here. This is the women's bathroom.'

'I know. I'm sorry to barge in here like this but I needed to talk to you.'

'I…I don't know you.'

She's scared. Of course she is.

'I'm a friend. I just need to ask you a question. Please… I don't mean you any harm.'

Linda shifts on the spot and turns off the tap. It's suddenly very quiet in the women's bathroom.

'I can't talk to you. My husband is right outside. Let me go to him or I'll scream.'

'I know Harry Preston.'

She stares back at me like a deer in the headlights.

'How do you know Harry?'

'He's not your husband.'

The tap drips.

'Who are you?' Linda asks. She's motionless now.

We are both frozen in time.

'I promise I'm not here to stop you. I just want to know why you and Harry are going to kill yourselves.'

Linda stares at me with the widest eyes imaginable.

'Tell me who you are.'

She's not going to let this go. I can't tell her about the time travel. It's too much information to drop on someone in a public toilet. I'm going to sound insane.

I have to improvise.

'I'm a psychic. I sensed you from outside the hotel. Please trust me.'

'If you're a psychic then you should already know why we want to die.'

I hold my fingers to my temples and pretend to strain.

'It's cloudy. I can see your hotel room on the second floor. You're breaking a pipe. There's a baby. Did you recently give birth?'

Linda clutches the catholic cross that hangs around her neck. She stares through me.

'I don't believe in psychics,' she starts, 'but… I am a woman of faith.'

'Please have faith in *me* then. Consider me a guardian angel.'

Linda blinks hard and places one hand on the sink to steady herself.

'And… you won't stop us? You won't speak to Harry?'

'I promise you. I just want to know what's going on. Will you talk to me? Please?'

She turns around and runs the tap to rinse the sink even though there is nothing in there to wash away. Linda looks embarrassed and takes a deep breath.

'I did just have a baby. A boy. He was beautiful.'

'Why did you leave him? Why are you running away?'

'I'm not running away. I can't be a parent.'

I want to know the truth.

'I'm…'

Say it.

'I'm dying.'

There it is. My worst fear confirmed.

'I'm so sorry,' I say as I fight back tears. I didn't expect to care so much about this woman that I hardly know but I'm overcome. The bathroom feels unstable like a waterbed beneath my feet.

'I have lung cancer. I'm a smoker and my lungs are shot.'

I suddenly have the urge to hug my mother and tell her that I love her but I resist.

'Is that why you want to die?'

'Yes I suppose. I could have had chemotherapy but I was pregnant. I wanted to have the baby and I didn't want to risk hurting him with radiation. I put it off and now it's too late.'

It's my fault.

'You know you don't have to do this. Harry could raise your son alone.'

'Harry loves me but he doesn't want to live without me.'

'Maybe if you talked to him…'

'No! This was his idea. He told me that if I die, he'd die. He means it too.'

'But surely now that he has a child?'

'Harry helped me through the labour and he was the first person to hold my son. He told me he didn't feel anything. He loves me, not our son. Harry doesn't want to be a father. He never did.'

So there it is.

This is the end.

I can't give the glove to my mother because she won't live long enough to use it. I can't give the glove to my father because he has a death wish.   I can't go back beyond my birth to a time when they were in a better headspace because the glove won't let me. If I try to go back I'll land at the moment of my birth and the ride will be over. No more time travel. I'll have to live out the rest of my life in this time knowing that I failed a long line of ancestors and that all of this was for nothing.

I have no moves left.

The sex that Ben and Lola are having in my mind is probably the best sex any two people have ever had. It is a combination of what I imagine is happening mixed with my fading memories of the night. I stay up meditating. I find sleep elusive but take it in patches here and there. The appearance of Ben means that we are nearing Helena's time of death. I'll have to watch her more closely and follow at a safe distance. By the time Ben leaves in the morning I'm dressed and ready to move. He doesn't look like a man that has just had a life changing experience. That realisation will come with time. This man still thinks he will see Lola again but he won't.

Ben drives away and Helena catches a taxi into the city. I follow in my cheap blue car at a distance. She looks into her rear view mirror and at times I'm sure she's looking at me. I'm so paranoid these days.

I find driving has always come easily to me. I drive defensively and follow Helena all the way to the movies. She buys a ticket and heads in. Poor Ben would have definitely blown off Uni and gone to the movies with her had he known. I park but don't bother to pay the ridiculous premium for kerbside parking before being pleasantly surprised by the cheap movie ticket prices of the past. There is only one film starting now so I get a ticket and head in. There are three of us in the cinema so I sit on the right side behind Helena. There are three rows between us. It's an art film but the music is beautiful. I spend the next two hours watching Helena watch the film. She cries towards the end when the protagonist dies and I feel so much empathy for her that I cry too. I am reminded that she is in grave danger and I cautiously watch the third patron. He's an old man and I wonder if he knew what this film was before he bought a ticket. Perhaps he's alone too.

When she leaves her seat Helena has to walk right past me to leave. Everything slows down as she moves up the aisle. For a perfect moment, a moment that I feel like has been months in the making; Helena looks at me and smiles with tears in her eyes. She smiles at me in a way that says *we shared an experience here*. My heart melts and I wish I could tell her everything. She brushes her blonde hair behind her ear and heads for the exit.

A movie moment at the movies.

Helena burns herself into my mind again. She is so effortlessly amazing. I've fallen for her and I can't get up. It's been so long since I spoke to anyone, let alone touched another person. I realise I'm smiling and I can't stop. My cheeks start to hurt as I finally leave the cinema. Helena is walking around slowly as if she is adjusting to the real world. It's bright. I linger at a nearby bookshop where a child stares at my gloved hand. I hide it in my pocket and turn back to watch Helena. She smells flowers at a florist. She chats to the female employee. She acts like she has all the time in the world even though the opposite is true.

When she finishes shopping she heads in the direction of her home. She decides to take a bus, which makes it difficult to follow her. I take my chances and drive my car ahead to meet her there. I'm relieved when I see her walking towards her door from my car.

That night I feel exhausted. My mind tells me to watch Helena and to protect her but my body is failing me. I estimate my age to be approximately thirty-five though it could be as high as forty. I don't know what forty is supposed to feel like. I'll never know exactly. I make a mental note to celebrate my birthday soon. I'm sure I haven't had cake in years either. Sleep and I fight like adolescent boys and eventually I lose.

In the light of day Helena goes out wearing sunglasses. She walks into a park and sits on a brown bench for a long time. She hasn't brought anything else with her except a handbag. I keep my distance and sit at the edge of the park facing the other way. I continually find reasons to turn around and watch her. She doesn't seem very upbeat today and she barely moves. What has changed? Did she get another phone call or a knock on the door that I slept through? I feel like I've missed something.

It's almost lunchtime and I consume some snack bars from my jacket pocket. I have learned to carry several items of food with me at all times as I often forget to eat. This stakeout of Helena has actually been very good for my waistline. My heart stops momentarily when a man sits beside her and snatches the sunglasses from her face. Though he looks familiar I'm not sure if he is one of the men I saw outside her place or whether I've seen him at *Secrets* before. He puts his arm around her and I can tell through his body language that they know each other. He must know her from the club. Since she fled with my younger self, Helena hasn't been back to work. I vaguely remember her fleeing that night. Was this the man she was evading? She doesn't make eye contact with him but he continues to talk at her. Helena clutches her handbag to her chest defensively. He reaches his right hand forward and pinches her cheeks between his fingers, forcing her to look at him. He has an intimidating face but doesn't resemble a thug. He reminds me of a video game boss. I scan the park and see several other men nearby. They are like generic video game goons, faceless and forgettable. He hasn't come here alone.

What does he want from Helena?

Did she quit her job or something?

Before too long he walks away and his bodyguards leave with him. The park is too public a place for any further action. They are biding their time but I can't wait anymore. I have to talk to her. Helena sees me coming and is frozen to her bench.

'Do you remember me?' I ask as I sit down.

She looks at me with fear in her eyes. At this moment I'm just another stranger approaching her in a park.

'Who are you?' she says searching my face for clues.

'I'm Brad,' I say without questioning whether or not she knows my true identity. I'm so used to my disguise that I feel like Ben is a completely different person even though we are the same. 'Are you alright?'

'I'm fine.'

Helena clutches her handbag. She's being defensive. I can understand that.

'Do you recognise me from the cinema? You walked past me the other day?'

She relaxes a little but says nothing.

'I saw that man talking to you. What did he want?'

'It was nothing. Just forget it okay?'

She's trying to keep me out of it. I'm just some Good Samaritan in a park.

'I can help you,' I say quietly. 'Do you need someone to talk to? Do you want me to walk you home?'

She gets up and starts walking away from me.

'Helena!' I call out suddenly. She turns around and stares at me. She's completely surprised that I know her name.

'Be careful.'

'How do you know me?' she asks. I can feel every inch of the space between us.

'I don't know you.'

'How do you know my *name*?'

'I live near you. I may have heard it around.'

'Bullshit. No one in my neighbourhood knows me. Where did you hear it?'

Maybe I should tell the truth.

The truth backfired when I told it to Ally.

But Helena is not Ally.

'I don't know you. We haven't met yet but you met Ben the other night.'

Her eyes stare straight into mine.

'I'm Ben… from the future.'

Helena starts walking away and I hurriedly follow her.

'Please stop. I'm trying to help you.'

'You expect me to believe you? Stop following me!'

'I knew you as Lola. You never told me your name was Helena.'

'You could have read my mail. You claim to know where I live. Hell, you claim to know the future!'

Dammit.

'Helena, someone is trying to kill you. I came back from the future to rescue you. Please believe me. I don't want anyone to hurt you.'

'So *who* is trying to kill me?'

'I don't know that yet. Could it have been that guy that was talking to you?'

'How am I supposed to know? I haven't been killed *yet* have I?' she says sarcastically.

'What did he say to you?'

Helena stops and I brace myself.

'You sound like an insane man. You need to stop this rubbish or I'm calling the police.'

Should I show her the coins? How can I prove this to her?

'I know. It's such a long story and I don't know how I can make you believe me.'

Suddenly it hits me.

The glove!

'Helena! Look at this glove. I *can* prove it to you.'

I touch my thumb and pinkie together creating the holographic orb in my palm. Helena stares dumbfounded and I realise that I must have looked just as stupid when Old Jack showed this to me.

'I wear this glove to travel backwards through time. If I take it off then I'll die.'

'How are you doing that?'

Helena's mouth is agape as she squints at the orb.

'It is technology from the future. I don't know exactly how it works.'

'So you're Ben? That I just slept with? You said your name was Brad?'

'Yes I know. It's confusing for me too sometimes. I call myself Brad now. It's an alias… like how you call yourself Lola. We slept together underneath a painting of a tiger with a peacock in its mouth. You gave me Viagra so I would last longer. You told me you got it from a girl at the club. I lost my virginity that night.'

She steps towards me and I shake the hologram away.

'I don't know how you know all this. You do look like Ben. You have the same eyes.'

She considers things for a moment and then folds her arms.

'I don't believe in time travel.'

'Helena, it's true. I'm here to save your life.'

'Show me.'

'Show you what?'

'Time travel. Show me,' she demands.

'I can't. The minute I go back through time you'll forget we ever had this conversation.'

'Then remind me again.'

'You might just end up wanting proof again. Then I'll be stuck in a weird time loop where I keep trying to prove to you that I'm telling the truth.'

'Okay, then I will tell you some things that only I know. Then when you tell it to me again I will know that you are telling the truth.'

'Alright.'

'When I was a girl in Russia and I graduated from school the teachers hired a band as a surprise for the students. When they congratulated us on finishing school the curtain was pulled back and the band played. There was such a sense of euphoria that all of the students ran up and danced like wild animals.'

'And that's a story that no one else knows?'

'What no one knows is that I didn't dance. I didn't move. I was sad to be leaving school. I didn't want to grow up. I was so scared of the future that I started to cry. My friend Costa asked me why I was crying and I told him they were tears of joy. I was crying because I was terrified. Costa could tell and he stayed sitting with me. Neither of us danced.'

Helena is shaking like a leaf in front of me. I don't know what to say.

'If you tell me that story I will know.'

'Thank you. That means so much to me. I want you to know that you have nothing to be afraid of. I won't let anything happen to you.'

'I don't know if *I* believe you,' she says with a nod, 'but I can see that *you* believe you.'

'What did that guy say to you? Please tell me. It might be important.'

'He works at the club... *Secrets*? Do you know this place?'

'Yes I remember the club,' I say quickly.

'He knows that I will dance but he has been trying to make me work at the brothel too.'

'He can't make you.'

'He can. He says if I don't work in the brothel then I have to shoot porno films.'

'You don't have to do *either* of those things.'

'If I don't he says he will report me. I am not supposed to be working while I'm in Australia.'

'You have to stop working there,' I plead.

'I have. I left there that night when I jumped in the car with Ben...with you.'

I smile. Maybe Helena is starting to believe me.

'Other girls have disappeared too. They are afraid. No one wants to be deported so they do as they are told.'

'I'll help you. If anything goes wrong I'll change things. I'll get it right.'

She looks at the glove and then her eyes dart back up at me.

'This is very strange. If it's true?'

'It's true.'

Helena touches my face for a moment. She stares into my eyes.

'So you still remembered *me*? After all these years?' she asks.

'They say you never forget your first time.'

We stand still and for a moment nothing else in the world matters.

'Ben is a cute boy. But you…you have grown into a very handsome man.'

'That's nice to hear.'

Helena gives me a nod.

'I'm leaving now.'

'Alright, thank you for talking to me Helena.'

She walks towards the large metal gates that border the park but keeps looking back at me every ten steps or so. I put my gloved hand in my pocket and wait for her to disappear almost completely out of sight before I start to follow her again.

Today I have to go downtown and unclog a toilet. It's the glamorous side to being a plumber that no one wants to know about. My IPad tells me that a child flushed a toy and it got stuck. It's autumn and the brown leaves make the whole world look the way I've been feeling.

Everything is still shit. I'm struggling to find the motivation to get out of bed. I haven't had a drink since I met the old man claiming to be from the future. In a weird way he kind of scared me straight. I've made the decision to try and force myself to be happy but Sam hasn't made it easy. She and Jack are home and I feel like a third wheel. That's why it's so great to go to work. Plumbing still makes me feel useful even if Sam doesn't.

The house is a two-storey brick house with a bright pink door. It's easily the nicest house on the street. I knock and a brunette opens the door.

'Hi I'm Ben. You called a plumber?'

'Hi, I'm Lucy. My daughter flushed her stuffed lion down the toilet and its clogged. Thanks for coming on such short notice.'

I wipe my feet before she leads me downstairs to a guest bedroom and en suite. The house is spacious and well kept. I thought she said she had a kid? This is immaculate compared to the bombsite I'm living in right now.

'The lion was a gift from my parents when she was born. I'm hoping you can save it?'

'I'll do my best.'

'Thank you. She's a Leo so she got lots of lion stuff. Do you have kids?'

'A boy. Jack.'

'Cute! How old is he?'

'Almost a month.'

'So new! Congratulations!'

'Thank you.'

'You shouldn't be back at work yet. You should be enjoying that new baby.'

'I don't mind really.'

And then I see it. In front of me I see a painting of a tiger holding a dead peacock in its mouth. I'd recognise it anywhere. It is the painting from Lola's house - the painting that hung above me when I lost my virginity. Suddenly I start to sweat.

I have stopped dead in my tracks.

How did this get here?

'This is going to sound crazy but I know this painting. Where did you get it?'

Lucy holds her breath. The atmosphere in the room instantly intensifies.

'A friend of mine painted it.'

'Lola?'

Her eyes go wide.

This is impossible.

'She... used to go by Lola...yeah.'

'How did you know Lola?' I manage to ask.

'How did *you* know her?' she fires back.

'I had sex with her. She was… my first.'

Lucy screws up her face.

'What was your name again?'

'Ben.'

'Lola never mentioned you to me.'

While Lola had always stayed on my mind it would seem that I was merely a footnote in her story.

'I spent one night with her and then she disappeared. Do you know where is she now?'

Lucy pauses before delivering the news.

'She died.'

My heart skips a beat. Everything seems to slow down for a moment as I try and process this new information. In my mind she's still so young and perfect. And alive.

How can Lola be dead?

'How did she die?' I ask.

'She was shot. They never found the killer. The police said it was random.'

I tell Lucy all about how I met her at the strip club and how she changed the direction of my life. Lucy goes on to explain the particulars of how her body was found and I realise that I must have been one of the last people to see her alive. I have to lie and tell Lucy that my encounter with Lola was weeks earlier than it was to avoid suspicion from her. She had been killed in the 24 hours after our night together. I can imagine the police interviewing me and reopening her murder case. I can remember all the details of my night with Lola but I'm not sure I can remember the hours afterwards or my alibi.

'And how did you know Lola?' I ask again.

'We used to work together at the strip club. We were close and when she died I cleaned out her place with some of the other girls. I wanted to keep something of hers.'

Lucy looks embarrassed. She's clearly put that part of her life behind her and doesn't want her husband and daughter to know about it. I look up at her face and it hits me. *Lucy is Willow.*

She jerked me off through my pants while giving me a lap dance. Holy *fuck*. She looks great. I feel like we are both turning red and I turn and focus on the painting again.

'She meant a lot to you huh?' Lucy says quietly.

'Yeah.'

After a pause she places a hand on my shoulder.

'Do you want the painting? If Lola really meant that much to you… I don't mind.'

Suddenly all I can think about is whether time travel is real.

'No thanks.'

I fix the toilet and save the lion. It has a horrible new smell but that's not my problem. Lucy doesn't recognise me and I don't say a word. I'm sure she gave thousands of guys lap dances over the years. I'm no one special in the scheme of things. Just like I wasn't someone special to Lola. I say goodbye and take a mental picture of the painting.

I have to go to the hotel and see Old Jack.

I drive my work van away from the house with the pink door.

I hope he's still there. I wonder if he's telling the truth?

He knew I'd hear about Lola and he was right.

I have to talk to him again.

The door is in one piece again. The chaos has been avoided. I'm floored by Harry's words.

We want to die.

He speaks for Linda as well. Without warning a woman steps out of the bedroom in a robe and screams when she sees me standing dumbfounded in her hotel living room. I roll my eyes at the absurdity of the situation.   I walk through the door and pulse away again. I can't afford to start this way. I need to be invisible.

I find Linda Kellerman's husband Michael Kellerman after bribing a series of people. People prove time and again to be easily corruptible. It seems she had an affair with my father and I was the product of that relationship. Michael Kellerman lives in a modest house in an average neighbourhood. He seems happy to speak to me when I tell him I'm a police officer. The inside of his house is full of pictures of my biological mother Linda. In every picture she smiles without showing her teeth. There is a child-like wonder in her expressions.

'I'm just wondering about your wife. Do you know her whereabouts?'

'I'm sorry no. She phones me sometimes and hangs up. She doesn't say anything but I know that it's her.'

'And when was the last time you saw your wife?'

'It's been almost a year.'

I sigh and realise he's been hoping she will come back.

He thinks they will be together again.

'Do you know a man by the name of Harry Preston?'

'Yes. What's this about?' he asks as he takes a seat on the sofa.

'How do you two know each other? If you don't mind me asking.'

'Socially. I know his wife Olive. I believe Linda and Olive were friends before Linda took off. I never really kept track of my wife's friends.'

'Mr. Kellerman, Harry Preston and your wife were seen in hospital together recently,' I blurt out knowing that he will never remember this conversation.

'What are you talking about?'

'Harry and Linda became parents to a baby boy only a few days ago.'

'So she's been with *him*? I'd been under the impression that she'd moved in with friends. That she needed some space! You're telling me that she has been with *Harry Preston*?'

'Yes, I'm afraid so.'

He sits incredibly still, struggling under the weight of this new information.

'My wife…' he says before trailing off.

He provides me with Olive Preston's address but before I head across town to break the news to her he stops me.

'Could I ask you one thing?' Michael asks as I'm approaching my car.

'Of course.'

'What…um…'

He furrows his brow and exhales.

'What did they name him? The boy.'

'Benjamin.'

It's a surreal moment but this man is no one to me.

I'm surprised when I see what a stunning woman Olive Preston is. It's hard to believe that anyone would ever leave her. She's much more in the loop than Michael was.

'Oh yes. I suspected the two of them were together. Harry told me he was leaving me for another woman. Said I had turned sour. To be honest I found his touch repulsive by the end.'

So it's all finally clear.

I *was* the result of an affair.

In my original timeline Harry and Linda, my parents, ran away together from their respective partners. They got pregnant with me, had me and then checked into a hotel with the intention of ending their lives.

I'm glad I never knew any of this before.

It's kind of a depressing origin story.

I will have to intervene again. I'll have to convince them of the truth. I know Old Jack didn't convince me the first time around either. He actually never had me completely on side and had to trick me in the end. It's a shame I can't give the glove to Olive or Michael. They seem like they would be willing to go back and have another chance at life. As I'm not related to either, the glove wouldn't work for them so I let the idea go as quickly as it arrives.

I head back to the Hyatt Hotel and prepare myself for another confrontation with my parents.

When I get back to Russia I'm forced to wait for Helena with her brother Oleg. We shuffle around the house avoiding each other. I plant a rose garden in the front yard. I start eating meals in my room and continue to learn Russian. It's a small gesture and I'm not very good but I hope it will serve as a reminder of my willingness to blend our two worlds. I send her a few texts and get short but promising replies. She'll meet me at the airport tomorrow.

I spot Helena amongst the crowd of people converging at the arrivals gate.

She looks as beautiful as ever.

'How was Amsterdam?' I enquire as I kiss her on the cheek.

'I smoked some weed, which I think might have been a bad thing,' she says looking down.

'If it helped you relax then it's probably okay,' I offer.

'It might have been bad because I'm pregnant.'

As she watches for a response my first thought is that this is a miracle. This must be the reason the glove was invented in the first place and now our child will save the human race somehow. Everything I've been through has been to impregnate this woman here and now.

Unfortunately the chances of this child being mine are next to none.

'Did you hear me?' she asks and forces a smile.

'Yeah. I heard you'

She doesn't know my sperm is useless. I confront her and ask directly if it's mine.

'Of course. You're my husband.'

'I don't believe you.'

This is apparently the worst thing I could say because Helena falls apart in front of me. She starts sobbing and I tell her about my tests and how I can't be the father. I tell her it would be nearly impossible odds.

'Then this is our miracle,' she says defiantly.

'I don't think you are having my baby. Be honest with me Helena. I don't deserve lies.'

After a minute of silence she confesses that it's not mine and that she's been having an affair.

'Who is he?' I ask, uncertain I want to know the answer.

'My friend Costa.'

Costa from the story she once told me. He was the one who comforted her when she cried at her graduation. When she was scared of growing up and facing the world.

How long has this been going on?

She told me she suspected the child was his and now thanks to this new information about my sperm she could confirm it. We cry a little but neither of us comforts the other. We have grown apart. We sit down at a nearby café to talk but it takes a long time before either of us does.

I don't have an appetite and ask for a glass of water and nothing more. Helena tells me about the man she loved before moving to Australia. She tells me about a man that she has never forgotten. He was a promising musician that never had his big break. Financially Costa couldn't afford to come and see her but they had an unspoken agreement that one day they would be together when the time was right. I think back to our shared lottery win and Helena's admission that she thought about running away.

She stayed with me as long as she could really. Lola was my dream girl but I was never her dream man.

Costa was.

I was a nice man to pass the time with and when I became rich it made everything easier. It made loving me easier. I realise now that the reason Helena moved us to Russia was to be closer to him.

How long had the affair been going on?

It didn't really matter anymore.

I think she had always intended to leave me eventually.

My mind wanders and I find myself thinking about Sam. I wasn't her true love either. I don't think I'm meant to be with anyone.

My life's purpose is to never exist.

I have to go back and give the glove to one of my parents.

'So what happens now?' Helena asks me quietly. A waitress walks by and gives us an angry stare.

'Do you want to be with Costa?' I ask only as a formality because I know the answer.

She nods.

Time stops and I wish I could be anywhere else.

'Forgive me. I never wanted to hurt you,' Helena says and touches my hand.

She wants a civil breakup. Maybe she thinks we can still be friends. I know now that this will be the last time I ever see my Helena. I will never remember my time with Lola in the same way again.

Time ruins everything.

We were never meant to be together and I forced it to happen. I have played God for the last time, bending the world the way I think it should bend.

Into a shape that pleases me.

I haven't time travelled in a long time. I'm too old to go back and repeat this all again. Helena would never go for me now.

I'm too old.

You can't make someone love you when they are in love with someone else.

I take a mental picture of this woman knowing she will never bear the child growing inside of her because I'm about to change the past yet again.

'I forgive you Helena. Goodbye.'

I activate the glove and in a blink everything changes. I've jumped back years without thinking. It's night and the airport café is still.

It is quiet now so I sleep.

When day breaks I rent a car and take a drive to Helena's parents' house.   I use the hidden spare key to let myself in. I creep into Helena's room and find a child of about eight or nine years old. She is still sleeping.

I can't have been the variable that ruined Helena's life.

She made bad decisions before she met me. She told me she was trouble after all.

She tried to warn me.

Here as a child she still has her mother and the memories of her father.

I want to remember her like this. Innocent and full of possibility.

It's time I went back to the greatest crossroad of my life. I need to meet my parents and find out why they didn't want me once and for all.

It's time to go back to the beginning, when I was innocent too.

I walk along kicking leaves out of position in a spacious park. I've spent a week meditating and reading while I try to come to terms with my situation but it's been hard to focus. Meeting my parents, a fantasy that I never thought would materialise, was the most devastating and soul-crushing moment I have ever experienced. My mother was at death's door and my father would rather die with her than raise me.

I suddenly feel like I've been orphaned all over again. It was almost better not knowing what happened to them.

I think about Helena and know now in hindsight that she was never the love of my life. I know Sam and I weren't right either. Of all the women I have loved throughout time there is no person I miss and no one that I wish was by my side now. You are born alone and you will probably die alone. Maybe Harry and Linda were right to end things at the height of their passion. They died before they could fizzle out. On their own terms.

Would I do it all the same?

Being an orphan crippled my view of a healthy family unit. I know in my heart that if Linda wasn't sick and she had raised me I would have been happier. My mother had a kind soul and I felt overwhelmed after knowing her for only a short time. I can only imagine what a lifetime of her influence would have been like. Harry would have been a tough father figure. Maybe he would have made sure my life had stayed on course. Maybe I would have ended up being a policeman after all. If Linda was to be believed he would have loved her forever. Maybe he would have softened over time. Maybe I would have had a little brother or sister.

It's each 'maybe' that haunts me now.

Maybe I should have known better.

Maybe I should have given my mother the glove anyway.

Maybe I should have tried to go back further.

Maybe the glove has other functions.

Maybe I'm the peacock in Helena's painting.

Helpless.

Dead.

Time travel allowed me to enjoy riches and a lifestyle that was beyond my imagination. I was able to sleep with more people than anyone alive. It ultimately taught me the value of personal relationships and the importance of family. Each time I pulsed away from my problems or tried to give myself a better life I had to start again. I had to leave everything behind. The phrase 'you can't take it with you' takes on a whole new meaning when you're tumbling through your past. You only really have your memories.

I have spent most of my waking hours thinking about Old Jack.

My son.

I think if I could stay alive long enough to see him pulse back and start this adventure again I would definitely have some more questions for him. Was he lonely? Did he have regrets?

Not raising him is my biggest regret.

It's a part of my life that I'll never truly know. He stole it from me.

I wish I had believed him and listened to him.

All the things I think I know about my son are really assumptions I have made over the years. We didn't spend enough time together.

This has made me see how important connections can be.

Everyone we meet and interact with changes from that interaction.

Ironically I turned out to be the same as my own father in a way. I didn't want to have a child with Sam. When Jack was born I felt nothing towards him in the same way Harry felt nothing towards me. Did I stay with Sam and help raise Jack? I'll never know. Was I a good father to him? I didn't ask. Where was I when Sam died? I'm saddened because I can never answer these questions and it keeps me up at night.

I don't want to die like this.

The cycle has to be broken but I know now that I'm not the one to do it. I've been through life and lost.

…

But this doesn't have to be the end of the story.

At this moment in time my parallel self is almost two weeks old.

In a way I have my entire life ahead of me.

I grew up the first time without parents and didn't reach my potential. But what if this time I had a father? A man that knew *all* the mistakes I was destined to make. A man that knew me better than I knew myself.

What if I raised myself to be better?

To be *more*.

I might not live long enough to see Old Jack again but I can make sure that Ben Stanley is prepared for the moment in his future when *he* does.

I can give him a better life. I can teach Ben all about the glove before he inherits it. And if I die I can leave him the glove with a book to explain it all. He can operate the glove because he *is* me.

I won't be dead if he is alive.

I'll live on.

It might be strange to him that as he ages he will grow to look more like me. Maybe I'll make things worse and ultimately ruin his life.

I can't anticipate failure.

I have to try.

I have to undo the damage that was done to me and come out the other side. I don't know if this will work or not but it feels like my best chance. What was the point of going through life if it doesn't help the next generation? I have to pass on what I've learned.

There is no 'magic button' solution. When you become an adult you don't know suddenly know how to 'do' life. That's why people still commit suicide, people get divorced, people believe in God. People need to think that there is something else bigger than them. People don't want to feel like a tiny cog in a huge machine.

I guess in the scheme of things Helena will forge her own path. I don't know whether my presence here in the past will change her story at all.   I suppose if the younger version of Ben never meets Helena then maybe she won't be shot in the street like that. I know I will be tempted to check in on her when it gets closer to her time. For now I have to be selfish.   I need to make sure that I don't repeat the mistakes of my past. I have to do a better job this time around.

It's a clean slate.

For the first time in a long time I'm filled with hope.

Ben will have questions for me and one day I hope I can answer them.

I'll tell him everything when he's old enough to handle it.

Time travel can be a real mind fuck.

As I drive towards the school I look up into the rear view mirror and see Ben staring back at me.

'What's wrong?' I ask.

'What if I don't like it? What if I don't make any friends?' he says.

I remember the wise words that Doug spoke to me on the morning of his wedding.

You can't just think about what could go wrong. You have to be open to the possibility that everything will work out for the best.

'Everything will work out for the best,' I tell him.

He stares out the window as I navigate the car into a nearby park.

I stare at the glove on my right hand. It looks as new as the day I first put it on. I know that nothing I do will mean anything if I use the glove again. This is my life now and the only useful function this glove now serves is to keep me here in my past. I exist outside of time.

I open the door for Ben and he nervously slings his bag over his shoulder.

'It will be more fun than you think,' I say and give him a hug.

'Maybe.'

'It's going to be amazing,' I offer with a smile.

'How do you know?' he asks.

'I just believe it.'

Ben gives me another hug.

'I'll be here at ten past three to pick you up.'

'Ok.'

'I love you Ben.'

'I love you too Dad.

A complete reset means that my mistakes will be undone. I remind myself that they *have* been undone because they haven't happened yet. Things will be different this time.

I watch Ben as he heads towards the school. A girl wearing her hair in pigtails says hello to him and they walk together.

He looks happy.

Ben stops at the door and gives me a mighty wave.

I wave back with my gloved right hand and he disappears inside.

Everyone we meet and interact with changes thanks to that interaction.

This time around Ben will have the tools to deal with whatever happens.

Together we're going to be fine.

About the Author.

David Farrell lives in Melbourne with his wife Tess and their children.

He has Directed two feature films and has a film Podcast called *Pod Me If You Can*.

His e-book stories *The Last Resort* and *Twelve* are available now on Amazon for the Kindle.

You can contact him @DaveFarrell1 on Twitter.